Andrew Cowan's first novel, *Pig*, won a Betty Trask Award in 1993 and was published in 1994, when it also won the Ruth Hadden Memorial Prize, the Author's Club First Novel Award, *The Sunday Times* Young Writer of the Year Award and a Scottish Arts Council Book Award. His second novel, *Common Ground*, was published in 1996.

Born in Corby and educated at Beanfield Comprehensive and the University of East Anglia, Andrew Cowan now lives in Norwich with the writer Lynne Bryan and their daughter, Rose.

Also by Andrew Cowan

Pig
Common Ground

Crustaceans

ANDREW COWAN

SCEPTRE

First published in 2000 by Hodder and Stoughton
A division of Hodder Headline
A Sceptre Paperback

The right of Andrew Cowan to be identified as the
Author of the Work has been asserted by him in accordance
with the Copyright, Designs and Patents Act 1988.

10 9 8 7 6 5 4 3 2 1

A CIP catalogue record for this title
is available from the British Library.

ISBN 0 340 71304 6

Typeset by Hewer Text Ltd, Edinburgh
Printed and bound in Great Britain
by Mackays of Chatham plc, Chatham, Kent.

Hodder and Stoughton
A division of Hodder Headline
338 Euston Road
London NW1 3BH

Lynne

ONE

December and one foot of snow. The thaw in the towns is becoming contagious now, spreading out by these roads to the coast. People are working. I saw a man beating the tyres of his tractor, clumps of ice falling. A boy with a shovel tramped into a barn. The farm-truck ahead is piled with beets. I suppose they are beets. I raise a finger from the wheel and glance in the rear-view to find you. Sugar beets, I say. Can you see?

But you wouldn't be interested. You'd be watching these fields, kneeling out of your strap like you mustn't, and your breath would be misting the window. I'd scold you of course, and you'd offer this view, the black-bordered whiteness, as though for me too it was some kind of gift. *See the snow, Daddy!* you'd say. After which we would argue. You'd whine and I'd shout. Even today I would shout – because I don't want you falling, because I've told you before . . . Ach.

I sneeze and switch on the radio and tune it to nothing. White noise seeps into the car. Cold air from the coast rushes the windscreen. The land here is so flat, the snow covers everything. It's forgetful and simplifying, though I know that somewhere beneath there are seeds and tubers and stalks, tediously waiting – only sleeping – and soon enough there'll be too much again. These days there is always too much.

I ease down on the accelerator. The wheels of the farm-truck slick through the wet on the road. A solitary beet stirs from the pile then tumbles. In another few yards we'll be bumper-to-tail – the bolts on the drop-gate are rattling – and when at last I pull out to pass I glance again in the mirror and for a moment there's no one behind me, and nothing ahead, but even that emptiness crowds me and again I am breaking, I am crying, and it seems there's no point in continuing. I don't know where I'm going, or what I am doing. The car slews and steadies and I bring it to a halt in the verge. Beads of meltwater roll down the windscreen; the farm-truck grows small in the distance. I turn off the engine. I clear my nose. In the ticking silence that follows I take out my tobacco, I whisper your name. Are you listening, Euan? I say. Can you hear me? I remember the cold hard press of your bedframe, the sunburn on your shoulders. Shall I tell you a story? I say. Euan? Is that what I should be doing now?

TWO

It begins with Ruth and December and one foot of snow. This is twelve years ago. We were art students then, not yet twenty, and hundreds of miles from home. Ruth came to my flat-warming with a tin of white gloss. She was the only guest I'd invited and she stayed for five days. She stayed, in a way, for twelve years.

The college was small, red-brick and provincial. Its only advantage was to be so close to the seaside. When finally I told my father – the sculptor, your grandpa – that this was where I'd be going he thought I was joking, or foolish. He doubted my seriousness. With his name, and his contacts, he could have helped me find better. He said this with a frown, uselessly prowling his studio, touching things, moving things, not daring to face me. Strands of smoke curled in the sunshine. He lit a second cigarette, the first still burning in the bowl he used as an

3

ashtray. The bowl was a gallery piece, a gift from the potter, but my father was always brutal about potters' pretensions: a bowl was a bowl. And this school, he exhaled, was only good for *ceramics*; they would turn *me* into a potter; or worse, a pottery teacher. And then, for the first time, grinding out both cigarettes, he shrugged and told me I had talent. I could take my pick, anywhere would have me. But of course I didn't believe him; I doubted his honesty. I thought he was embarrassed to have suggested using his influence and would rather praise me than allow that to stand. So when suddenly his eyes flared out at me, his sculptor's eyes, as if I too were a piece of metal he could twist into shape, I let myself slouch back on the wall and gazed idly past him. He gave a tight shake of his head. He had nothing more to say to me.

I didn't send him my new address. He never wrote anyway and wouldn't have used it. The flat was in an attic, six flights of steep narrow steps to reach it. The stairs had no carpets, and neither did my two rooms. I moved in the day our first term ended, impatient to be free of my lodgings and the scrutiny of my landlady, her constant fussing around me. Now I paid rent to an agency, and could wash my own clothes, cook my own meals. I had no need of mothering. I had no need, I'd decided, of anything much. Before Ruth arrived that first evening I took down the curtains and threw out the lampshades. Whatever couldn't be hidden – packed into cupboards or pushed under the bed – went downstairs to the bins. Then I began on the painting. I wanted everything white – the skirting, ceiling, doors, walls and window-frames; all of it white. Ruth said it would look like a prison cell, which wasn't what I intended. More the opposite, I said.

The smaller of my two rooms was the bathroom. On our first morning we woke to find whorls of fern-frost on the inside of the windows, thin platelets of ice in the toilet, three inches of water in the bathtub. It had seeped up through the plughole. When later I heated the boiler, the pressure on the hot tap was so low, and the enamel in the bath already so cold, that the water barely rose above tepid. The tub was anyway too small to submerge in, and not nearly big enough to share, so we washed instead from a plastic bowl in front of the living-room fire, and shivered even there.

My kitchen – a sink, drainer and Baby Belling cooker – was built into a recess to the left of the chimney-breast, a slatted partition to hide it. The pillow end of the bed occupied the alcove to the right, a wall-mounted cupboard above it, a foldaway table and chairs underneath, and each morning for five days I dragged out this table and set it next to the window, then cooked up some breakfast and coaxed Ruth from the bed with a blue-hooped mug of black coffee. She sat wrapped in a blanket, her head just touching the slope of the ceiling, and smiled as I served her. The sea was grey in the distance, the snow softly falling, and afterwards we made love until lunch-time.

In the afternoons we decorated, and as we worked we listened to music. Ruth had brought a bundle of tapes in her rucksack, their plastic cases discarded. It was classical stuff mostly, and cinema soundtracks, and very old jazz; nothing I liked much. She'd made the recordings at home, with a microphone propped to the solitary speaker of her record player, and I could hear her feet as she crossed her bedroom, the door opening and closing, her footsteps returning. Sometimes there were voices, buses passing under her window, small shufflings and knocks, and always the hum of the speaker. It was this background noise that I listened to, as if pressing my ear to a wall, attentive to a life I couldn't see, trying to imagine. Then came the fumble and click at the end of each tape, when the Ruth at my side would lay down her brush and say, Fag-break, and we'd sit facing each other in front of the fire, our fingers spattered with paint, her tobacco and papers between us. She was teaching me how to roll cigarettes. We placed them on the hearth in two separate lines, hers smooth and regular, mine too fat or too thin, always lumpy or conical. The work was absorbing, compulsive, and we didn't say much. We didn't smoke, either. Smoking for me was secondary to learning to make them, whilst Ruth rarely lit hers till the evening, when we'd sit up on the mattress, our backs to the wall of the alcove, and talk.

There was a television. It stood on a trolley at the foot of the bed, the dull grey of its screen showing our reflection, a faint furring of dust on the glass. The set was dead, and eventually I'd wheel it out to the landing, but for those first few evenings we gazed at it anyway, and gossiped, and told funny stories, and compared our likes and dislikes, and nosed into each other's childhood. Ruth was reticent, but I learned of a mother she said she disliked, and a guiltily indulgent father she seemed to despise. He had left them for another woman when Ruth was thirteen, and was now, for a second time, unhappily married. She had no brothers or sisters, and neither of her parents, she implied, was interesting to her; she yawned when I pressed her, or became flippant, or changed the subject to me.

She had a way of asking me questions. Her eyes were huge, the blue-green of the irises almost entirely encircled by white. With the arch of her eyebrows, she often looked startled, or dazzled. But when she focused her gaze, as she had done the first time we spoke in the college canteen, the effect was unnerving – too keenly interested, too brightly attentive, and although this was flattering, and arousing, it also made me self-conscious. I stumbled over the simplest words. And yet, as she pried her way into my past on that bed, Ruth lowered her gaze, lowered her eyelids, and concentrated instead on her cigarette, the flecks of paint on her overalls, the weave of the bedspread beneath us. She doodled absently with a fingernail on my thigh, my arm, the back of my hand. Sometimes she took both my hands in hers and stroked them. She laid her head on my shoulder. And her voice was tentative, small, gently guiding me

7

to say more than I intended, more than I thought I remembered. She wasn't the first girl I had slept with, but she was the first I'd described myself to in such detail.

We were discussing my mother – speculating, supposing – when finally I smoked my first cigarette. I asked Ruth to light one, and she casually passed me her own, then lit up another. But I couldn't decide how to hold it, and in my awkwardness I recalled something more: an argument and the slam of a door, the chill of our staircase as I descended, and my mother standing alone in our kitchen, trembling, one arm poised as though lifting a glass, tilting her chin as if something might spill, but this time not drinking. She was smoking a cigarette, one of my father's, and it seemed misplaced in her fingers. She inhaled sharply, defiantly, three or four draws, then stubbed out what remained with an agitated flap of her hand, dispersing the smoke as she hurried towards me. Her eyes were raw – she was starting to cry – but I wasn't to worry; she cupped her hands round my face and said I wasn't to worry. I must have been five – no older than five – and I wouldn't see her smoking again.

As I told this to Ruth I felt my forehead and chest prickling with sweat. My heart, I realised, was racing, and suddenly in that white room the light was too bright, there was too much to see. I lay flat on the bed and closed my eyes. I thought I was going to be sick and when I got to my feet the giddiness made me lurch sideways. Ruth took the cigarette from my hand and followed me through to the bathroom. She sat on the rim of the

8

tub. Nicotine, she explained; it's a poison. But you'll get used to it. Which I did, soon enough.

Ruth had no interest in reading, but in her rucksack she carried a tattered collection of crosswords and sometimes, when we tired of talking, she would pore over these whilst I sketched her. I began from her eyes, or her nose, or her mouth, but rarely got further. I offered her fragments, so closely detailed she looked twenty years older. Then she'd draw me as rapidly as the artists who worked the seafront in summer. With one of her roll-ups between my lips I said I felt like someone other than myself, and she told me I looked unlike myself too, which wasn't unpleasant. Later we took photographs – of ourselves and the flat. Ruth had a camera on loan from the college, and would develop the film in the following term, her first time in a darkroom. The prints have steadily faded – she got the chemicals wrong – but the shots we took of each other were never meant to be likenesses. With half a film still remaining we stood before the cracked bathroom mirror and altered our faces with Sellotape. A long length flattened my nose. Another pulled hers upwards. I was trying to make her look ugly, I said, but couldn't. She tacked my eyes open wide, fixed my mouth to a snarl that she said was a smile, and then we photographed our reflections, the crack in the glass disfiguring us further.

What was left of the decorating we did the next morning. Then to celebrate we went out in a blizzard, tramping through snow that came to our knees, until we found a shop selling mince-pies. We helped ourselves to a bottle of milk on a doorstep. The cream was frozen, the silvered top perched on a column of flakes. Solid tubes of ice descended from drain-pipes, glassy spikes hung down from the gutterings, the bus shelters and railings, and we saw no other people. Back at my flat the fire had gone out. We pumped our last coins in the meter and switched on the boiler, draped our wet clothes on the tank and climbed into bed. We made love in a litter of pie crumbs, and Ruth fell asleep in my arms. I learned then how she snored. Outside the snowfall was dwindling, the sun almost shining.

It was mid-afternoon when we packed. The coach station was less than a mile away, and we left in no hurry, our rucksacks bulky with laundry, weighted with presents. Ruth was going to stay at her mother's; my holiday would be spent with my grandmother. We walked along roads emptied of traffic, vacant hotels on each side of us, and I remember the leathery creak of our boot-treads, snow piled at the kerbsides, and Ruth's gloved hand in mine. We spoke very little. A woman passed in the opposite lane, tugging a small girl on a sleigh, her face pinked with the cold, and when she smiled hello we didn't think to respond. We turned instead down a side-street and descended a hill to a park – the municipal gardens – where we dumped our bags on a bench and sat for a while looking out at the boating lake. The water was frozen, a fresh felting of snow on its surface. A few children played round the edge. Their parents walked on, paused and called and walked on. Dusk crept in from the sea, and I watched as a couple of boys skimmed a football across the width of the lake, kicking it backwards and forwards between them, streaking the snow, until finally it bobbled and spun to a halt in the centre. I fumbled under my cuff for my watch. It was time to move on and I hooked one arm through the straps of my rucksack, then heard someone shouting, a woman urgently running, and looked up to see a small boy on a tricycle. He was pedalling out to recapture the ball, already yards from the bank, and as I stood from our bench, half resolved to run down, I heard the click of Ruth's camera. It's the final shot on the film, and the boy is still there, a line of frost-shocked trees behind him, a sheet of thin ice beneath, and the ball forever a few yards away. That, too, was the twenty-second of December – three days before Christmas, your birthday – and no harm could ever come to him.

THREE

You sometimes return in the night. I sleep thinly. I hardly know myself to be dreaming. Hours pass. There's the flat, predictable flow of my thoughts, the sluggish recall of another day in your absence. All is routine, nothing uncanny. I hear a phone ringing but don't answer it. The kettle boils and I watch it. A bus pulls towards me and I make no move to get on. And then you are there. You make yourself visible. The numbness of my waiting dissolves and suddenly I know more than one expression, more than one emotion. There is joy, and the ache of wanting to hold you, but you keep your distance, your separateness from me. This is as much as you will offer, and yet still I cannot stop smiling. I peer at you closely, trying to absorb – to remember – every detail of your appearance. But even as my gaze touches your face, it blurs and you fade, your likeness eludes me. I click my tongue; I concentrate harder. I focus perhaps on your mouth, or your fringe, or your nose. I ask you to help me; I joke and cajole. But I know I am losing you. And then you are gone. My legs give way beneath me, a blanketing weight falls over me. There is panic, and the puncturing pain of my longing. Fragments of light glint near my eyes, silica-fine and piercing, and my body shakes uncontrollably, my blood becomes turbulent. I hear the sea crashing, receding, windbreaks flapping. Voices are calling, viciously whispering. A dog barks. Electrical connections fizz loose in the fairground; a single note blares from the carousel organ. I try to shout for someone to help me, but I'm suffocating – can't make any sound – and I twist and arch to escape, then realise that I've been here before. I know I am dreaming, but the agitation is real and will surely kill me; I shall die before I open my eyes. I grab for Ruth's arm, dig my nails in to rouse her, dig deeply, and keep digging until my nails break, until I remember it's already too late, that there's no point in continuing.

When I wake my body is heavy on the bed, the sheets undisturbed, everything quiet. I haven't moved, Ruth isn't beside me, and my breathing is steady. But something of the disturbance remains, and I know that whatever I now look at is likely to move, become animate, unpredictable. I don't fear it. I stare into the shadows and corners, all the low spaces. I will your image to form, I wait for you to appear, but I see only what I wish to forget. I get up and wander the house, switching on lights as I move from one room to the next, and I feel your presence then, more real than dreaming. You are in the passages, the doorways, all the in-between places. You evade me, slip away as I approach. But I know you are there, and I talk to you, I talk to you endlessly.

FOUR

I remember a moment just after you were born. The midwives were busy with Ruth, washing her down, unplugging the wires, and I wandered into a corridor to stand a short while alone. It was as good as any place to be – peaceful, spacious, uncluttered – though a smoker would have had to search longer. There were *No Smoking* signs everywhere. I breathed and exhaled, the air was suddenly full of you. And I thought, Who am I now, and what can I show you? I stared at the palms of my hands, the empty hands of your father, and I made myself promise never to hit you; I made myself promise never to leave you. I trusted in promises then. I was what you had just made me, and my thoughts ran to the seashore in summer, absurdly, too hastily, for I knew the names of nothing we might find there, but already we were gathering shells, casting stones at the waves, raiding rockpools for crabs. *Crustaceans.* I knew that word at least, and I helped you pronounce it.

Of course my hands had no idea then of the work you would find them. Today, in this cold, with your coat plumped out by your scarf, they would strain to fasten your toggles and I would scowl at your restlessness, the effort just to make you stand still. I would shape a tissue for your hand and guide it to your nose, show you how to pinch as you blew. I would kneel and turn you around and demonstrate once more how to tie the knots in your laces. Then I'd count the fingers into your gloves, ease the rim of your hat over your ears, and hold you by the shoulders and smile. So many things you wouldn't want to be shown, and which you wouldn't have time for.

But I was always too keen to instruct you, and too conscious by far of the life you'd grow out of. Whatever you wouldn't remember or notice, I made it my job to preserve. Nothing should be lost or discarded or buried. At first Ruth was indulgent – she saw the fear in all my behaviour – but she later grew wary. As if it wasn't enough simply to be there, your father, it seemed I must also become your curator. I treated you like history. In the weeks before you were born I packed a small suitcase with jars and cartons and tins from the supermarket, a capsule of brand names and packaging I wouldn't let you see till you were older; much older. I bought a copy of every newspaper published on the day of your birth, then added a videotape of that evening's news on TV. I kept the plastic bracelets that identified you to the nurses, and the shrivelled stem of your umbilical cord. I filled a shoebox with the cards and letters of congratulation that arrived in the first weeks of your life, and added to this the microtape from our answering-machine, another half-dozen messages, including one from my grandmother, who died before she could meet you. In Ruth's old rucksack I saved the toys and books you seemed most attached to, and some of the clothes we most liked you to wear. I kept a memento of each of your birthdays, and a souvenir from each of our holidays. I photographed you constantly, and sifted through every drawing and painting you made, adding captions and dates, and filing all of this neatly with your nursery-school workbooks in a banker's box in our attic. And then, in a black-and-red notebook, twelve inches by eight, I registered each small leap in your development – the age you sat upright, abandoned your pushchair, copied your name – until the changes were too many and too subtle and I decided at last I could trust to your own memory.

For a while I was able to recite the entire extent of your vocabulary. There were thirty or forty mispronounced words, and I listed them all on a page in the notebook – *abo* for apple, *banki* for blanket – each one dated, explained, and spelled as you spoke it. Your word for my hands was *hams*, and this at least I could share with Ruth, who had used the same word herself, lying beside me on that bed in my flat eight or nine years before. My hams. They were, she'd said, splaying the fingers, the worst thing about me. Sexual attraction for Ruth always began with the hands, and she preferred them smooth and unknotted, slim-fingered, unblemished – more like a young woman's in fact; much like her own. And mine were like spatulas, like shovels, too broad and too square. Also too pudgy, too knobbly, too blotchy. But they'd do, she assured me, pressing my palms to her cheeks and holding them there; they'd pass. She found their ugliness endearing, I supposed, another excuse to feel sorry for me, and I was relieved when later she called them dextrous, a reference to my performance with clay on the wheel, though meaning, I hoped, much more than that.

Years afterwards you examined them just as intently, hunkering beside me on the floor of my studio. I'd collected you early that day from nursery, as I often did then on a Friday. You had your own corner, your own tools and clay, and I would fire whatever you brought me, no matter how formless, how far from completion. Which was my promise to Ruth – not to try to teach or correct you – though I knew from the start that you'd never allow me. You wouldn't be shown, hadn't the patience for lessons, and of course you rarely stayed long in your corner. Every task I began became a game that involved you. Completing my paperwork, my orders and invoices, you would sit by my side with some forms of your own and scrawl through them. As I tidied my cupboards, my benches and shelves, you'd want to drag out the boxes, the sieves and stacked buckets that were stored underneath them. When I loaded my kiln you'd insist on playing with the props, stilts and cones; any clay I prepared would be decorated with gouges, lumpy additions, your name. But I didn't much mind this. It was enough to have you around, for those few hours of my week, in the place where I worked. I liked you to see me, busy at something, your father, and when you wandered away, as you regularly did – down the white plasterboard corridors, looking for places to hide, other studios to visit – I would find that I missed you, the work that you caused me.

My neighbours, mostly painters and printmakers, gave you sandwiches, crisps, crayons and pastels, strips of bubble-wrap, postcards. You were, everyone told me, no trouble at all. You called them your friends, even remembered their names, and often when you came back you'd be carrying another clutch of scrap paper, some more paintings and drawings to add to the sheaf in your corner. But that afternoon you didn't want to go out, and you didn't once interrupt me. You cut a ball of red clay into pieces and carefully arranged them in order of size, then planted a tool in each one. You lay on your belly and drew a picture for Ruth, another for me. You sat for some time with your drink, staring at nothing, and then decided to empty my bowls of pebbles and shells onto the floor, my bucket of grog and my sand, and pretended you were alone at the seaside. My 260 square feet of studio became our caravan, our beach. At home in yourself, I might not have been there. For half an hour then, all my other chores done, I sat up at my wheel – where I'd been working all morning – and though I switched on the motor, and slapped some more clay on the disc, I did nothing, but watched you. Miming and talking, and constantly moving, you were, I gathered, an orphan. You picked through the mess at your feet, looking for objects of interest – treasure and crabs, imaginary creatures – and you explained them as I would, to another just like you. I heard my voice in yours; and Ruth's, her exclamations. I slipped down from my seat and squatted beside you. Pretend you're a daddy, you told me, and nodding, I laid a small shell on my palm. It's a periwinkle, I said; is it a good one, Euan? Not *so* bad, you said, and dropped it back on the floor. You shuffled closer. You asked to look at my hand, and studied it closely, tracing your fingers over the bumps, the clay that was etched in the creases.

It was always my habit to use too much water when throwing. The clay became liquid, a wet glove to each wrist, and as the moisture evaporated it left behind a grey sediment, pallid and papery, which broke as it dried along the grain of my skin. Even after I'd washed, the grey would remain. And as you looked now at those lines, something occurred to you. What is it? I said, and you asked me my age. You were by then not merely four, but four and three-quarters, and age was important. Just as each house must have a number, so too must people, and mine was a three and a nought. Did that mean, you wanted to know, that I was going to die soon? No, not for a long time, I promised; not till I was very much older. But I was already old, you informed me, still holding my hand. You offered it up to me. See the lines, Daddy, you said. See the grey? Your voice was concerned, but consoling, and I wasn't to worry. It's only *quite* old, you told me, not *really* old. I think you're right, I smiled, and cupped both my hands round your face. My mother was twenty-five when she died. It was only a number. I patted your arm and said we ought to clear up: Ruth would be expecting us home soon.

More than a year has now passed since that afternoon, half a year since I last worked in my studio, and my hands are once again empty – idle, redundant – but for this one simple routine: I reach for my tobacco and papers. I hold the pouch in my left palm and pinch out some fibres. I draw them down the V of a Rizla, spreading and tamping, untangling the knots. I nip away the excess and return it to the packet. I put the packet aside. I roll the tobacco in its channel of paper, my hands almost touching, my head bowed and steady, as close here to the posture of prayer as I will now ever come. Then the momentary pause, and the tuck of my thumbs as I fold the Rizla in on itself and quickly smooth it out to a cylinder. I lick and seal the gum, fit the cigarette to my mouth and reach for my lighter. I touch the flame to the tip and breathe down the first smoke, then slowly exhale. And I wonder, would these hands seem older or younger to you now, Euan; nearer or further from dying? No trace of clay-dust remains, no layer of grey, but there are stains – amber-brown and persistent – on the pads of my thumbs, at the tips of my first two fingers, in between each of the knuckles. Which is something, at least, I never meant you to see, that your father never intended to show you. And one promise I failed to keep.

I glance up through the smoke at the mirror and turn the key in the ignition. The seaside is less than thirty minutes away.

FIVE

My mother was leading me to my grandparents' house. It was summer and the pavements were chalky, the hedges swollen in sunshine. I noticed the moss dividing the paving slabs, scuff-marks on my sandals, tiny insects. I picked up an Embassy coupon to give to my father, and paused by the wreck of an abandoned ice-cream van. All four of its tyres were flat. It had been there for months, a familiar landmark, more visible to me then than the tower blocks around it. The clack of my mother's heels drew me on. We were in a hurry, it seemed, though she never once said so. I ran to catch up with her, but she remained always ahead of me, hardly even aware of me. When finally we came to a main road – heavy trucks streaming past us and a smell of exhaust, streets of older housing beyond – she forgot to offer her hand. I had to remind her. As we stepped from the kerb I noticed the scrubbed rawness of her knuckles and the mauve indentation where her ring should have been. Her grip briefly tightened and I looked up to her face. Her eyes were hidden behind sunglasses. She wore a polka-dot headscarf, pink lipstick. When we reached the far side she released me.

My grandmother, tall and thin and wearing an apron, was cleaning the outside of her windows. Stretching upwards, she looked over her shoulder and made a face of surprise, more puzzled than pleased. She came to meet us at the gate and I went straight indoors to her living room. The darkly varnished door of the sideboard was slightly ajar, inside a smell of tobacco and beeswax. I found the biscuit tin and took it through to the kitchen, where I sat at the table and waited, the blue-painted wall directly before me, my grandparents' chairs to each side. After a while I arranged the sauce bottles on the oilcloth to hide the blemishes and stains. Beneath my elbows the pattern of flowers was fading, almost scrubbed out. Eventually I heard voices approaching around the side of house. The doorway darkened as they came in, and then my mother bent to embrace me. She kissed the top of my head and quietly said, I'll come for you later, be a good boy; and I nodded. After she'd gone my grandmother gave me a biscuit and poured out a beaker of barley water. She watched as I drank it. Then she went back to her chores and I played alone at the rear of the house, the upstairs windows blankly reflecting the sky.

It was several days before I saw my mother again. I

remember the green of the hospital gardens, the lawns close-cropped and spongy, the hedges as tall as my father. He stood near my grandad in the shade of a tree, the soil bare beneath them, their shoes darkly polished. They were smoking, facing away from each other. Two of my aunts and my grandma sat on a bench in the sunshine, speaking in murmurs. A cream-coloured ambulance was parked by the flower-beds. The driver wound down his window and took off his cap, raked a hand back through his hair. The red-brick of the hospital buildings resembled the bay-fronted terrace where my grandparents lived. Above the orange roof-tiles the sky was cloudless and blue. For some minutes I searched the shadowed interior of the hedges for insects, and found instead the denser mass of a bird's nest. When I lifted it out I scratched the back of my hand. Inside were a few fluffs of down, but no eggs, and I carefully replaced it. A couple of nurses strolled past me, smelling of perfume, their watches pinned upside down to their tunics. They smiled. My father stamped out his cigarette. He called me to follow him.

The light inside the hospital was gauzy, the walls painted white and pale green. A nurse strode ahead of us, splay-footed, her shoes as clumpy and black as a man's. I noticed red buckets of sand, rows of metal pans in a storeroom. A tall bony man in pyjamas shuffled to a halt in the corridor and waited until I had passed him. A woman in slacks and white clogs touched my head as she stepped round me. Then we entered a ward of elderly men and I heard a voice calling, Here she comes now, everyone rise! The nurse said something short in reply, and one of the men gave me a wink. He was laughing. The blue cast of his cheeks turned a shade darker and he folded his arms on his chest. I stalled by the foot of his bed and he reached to his side for a bag of boiled sweets. I went cautiously towards him, and heard another voice say, He's come over all shy. The old man shook a sweet by the twist of its wrapper, and when I snatched it away his laugh came as a wheeze, then he started to cough. The nurse and my father were waiting by the next double doors. The floor squeaked as I ran.

My mother had a room to herself, wide and tall-ceilinged, cool and uncluttered. A large enamel sink stood by the window. A block of bright sunlight fell just short of the bed. She smiled weakly across the distance between us and extended an arm, inviting me closer. I felt the pressure of my father's hand on my shoulder. Her nightdress was pale blue and puffed at the sleeves, scooped low at the front. Her wrists seemed too puny, her chest too exposed. There were flakes of dry white skin on her lips. My father began talking, and though she appeared to be listening, her attention never once left me. Her gaze was kindly but feeble, like an old lady's, and I stood where she wouldn't be able to touch me. My father mentioned the sweet I'd been given, and I opened my mouth to show her, but she didn't respond. She stared at the scratch on my hand, and frowned as though confused or annoyed, a single sharp crease in her forehead.

Then came the slow pooling of her tears. She turned her cheek to her pillows and looked at the wall. It was time to withdraw. My father led me back through the door.

In the weeks that followed I went with my grandparents to the seaside, and visited London with my father, and spent several days more in the company of Rene, his sister, until finally, one afternoon, I came home to find my mother again in our kitchen, a patterned pink blouse knotted under her ribs, rubber gloves on her hands, and the washing-machine churning. It was as though she had never been away, or at least, never would again. Yet I know, because I've been told, that she was to return to the hospital within a few days, her fourth time in less than a year. And on that last occasion, too, there was sunshine and I played unconcerned in the gardens, exploring the hedges, watching the nurses, though I didn't accompany my father indoors. When eventually he emerged from one of the buildings, seeming dazed by the sunlight and walking forgetfully, my uncle Ron came up behind him and placed one hand round his shoulder, the other supporting his elbow. I remember we filed in procession past the signboards, the porters' lodge and the flower-beds, and as we came through the main gates I saw the stalls of the market ahead of us, the council buildings beyond that, and complained we were going the wrong way, I'd been promised we would go to the park. My aunt Rene had lifted me into her arms and from the height of her shoulder I saw the blankness and bewilderment in the faces around me, my grandfather supporting my grandma, my uncle guiding my father, and I asked, Where's Mummy, when is she coming? To which there was no answer then, and for weeks and months afterwards, no answer from anyone.

SIX

I was warned about driving, cautioned against it. The mind wanders. For twenty miles this road to the coast meets no obstructions, no complications. It goes only there. But then come the trailers and chalets, the camping and caravan parks, and I took a right turn, came out where I hadn't intended to be. We're still heading for the sea, but the wrong side of the resort, towards my flat and the art school, away from our caravan.

I have come this way too often before. The town is fringed here by marshes, allotments, donkeys and ponies in ramshackle stables. A black-girdered bridge takes us over the river, quayside derricks in the distance, the flourmill and brewery. I accelerate past warehouses, squat industrial sheds, and arrive at the racetrack. Outside the stadium are hoardings of stock cars and bangers. The colours are gaudy, surprising. A grey canvas banner says *CANCELLED*. Fifty yards further on I turn left off a roundabout and ascend towards bungalows, pampas grass in the gardens, trees and hedges made blotty with snow. An old man walks with one hand outstretched for a fall, touching the lampposts, the railings. A car pulls cautiously out from a driveway. I pass turnings for crescents and closes, ice corrugating the road at the junctions, and come alongside a playground, where I slow without thinking, to avoid or see what I don't know. The pavements are empty, the wire enclosure deserted. A solitary gull heads for the roofs of the old town.

Near the crest of the rise are the houses with portholes, pink and blue walls, and a sign for the college, which is five streets below. Descending, I recognise everything sharply, the upward tilt of the sea, half-timbered hotels with fibreglass awnings, the pubs. At night, unable to sleep, I have traced the map of this route in my mind, the exact sequence of shopfronts. On the next corner comes the laundromat, its green conical roof sprouting a weathervane, a fat metal artichoke, and there I indicate left and follow a dark twist in the road, flint walls on both sides, and emerge to a car-park where a digger stands idle in a space marked by bollards. The gravel is swollen with ice. I make a wide circle and stop a yard short of the boundary trench, directly facing the college. In your first summer we came here, took photos of you in my lap on those steps, in your buggy with Ruth on that corner. Carved over the entrance in blocks of blackening sandstone are the words

T.E.C.H.N.I.C.A.L. I.N.S.T.I.T.U.T.E. and the date *1906*. The high narrow windows, barred now at street level, were always that grimy. I work my arms into my coat and gather up my tobacco and papers; my hat, scarf and gloves. From here I will walk. I push open my door to the cold, and remember my tissues, my cough sweets. I leave the car without locking it.

The college of course proved no better than my father had said it would be. To his mind, I knew, this town would always mean holidays, deckchairs and beachballs, frivolity. Nowhere so marginal, so close to the sea, could lead to anything solid or lasting. But most things about me then seemed to provoke him, testing his patience, his comprehension. Nothing I ever said could change that. I hardly bothered to try. I was putting myself out of his reach, the weight of his expectations. I had no other ambitions.

The engineering departments – marine, mechanical, agricultural – occupied most of this building, the wide flagstoned corridors smelling of oil and burnt gases. Art was taught in a wing at the back, and although the students there were visibly different, and kept themselves separate, the courses they followed were no less applied or vocational. The prize for best work in graphic design was sponsored by a greetings-card company. The ceramics department, where I spent my three years, was run along factory lines. It occupied four rooms in the basement, giving on to a courtyard, whilst sculpture, for which Ruth had enrolled, was dispersed throughout the building and its prefab extensions, never finding space enough anywhere. We met daily in the canteen, in the long queue for lunch, and always sat as a couple. That anyway seemed to be solid, and lasting.

Soon after our first Christmas apart, sitting knees touching in the clatter of pans from the kitchens, a tin-foil ashtray between us, I said, I've got something for you, and slid a Yale doorkey towards her. Ruth watched it approach, let it remain where it lay. It's a key, I said, and she nodded. You don't have to take it, I said; not if you don't want to, but I'd like you to have it. The brass teeth and notches were shiny. Only if you want to, I said. She drew on her cigarette, narrowing her eyes at the smoke, and then slowly, exhaling, she picked it up from the table. Thank you, she said, and shifted around in her chair. She crossed her legs and tucked the key in the back pocket of her overalls. Her knees had left me, but she was smiling, and I talked excitedly then about nothing in particular, what I'd been doing that morning, who I had seen, all the while hoping she'd speak, say something to stop me. But she did no more than smile, and the key wasn't mentioned again until she used it, four or five days after that.

It was the rasp in the lock that woke me. I opened my eyes to a blur of pillow and bedclothes, sunlight on the wall, and listened as if eavesdropping to the close of the door, her slow steps on the boards, the heavy fall of her coat. A long zip unfastened and she kicked off her shoes; the bed creaked as she climbed in and I rolled over to face her. It was a Saturday. She was wearing wool tights, a singlet, and my key round her neck on a cord of brown leather. She dangled it before me, tickled my nose. It fits, she said, and pulled the blankets over our heads. She smelled of outdoors. I burrowed half-way down the mattress, curling my legs around hers, and pressed my face to her belly. I could hear her breakfast. She tugged at my hair. I peeled her tights from her hips and went lower.

After that she would use her key whenever she called, and each time I felt as if waking. The hours I spent alone in my flat have left no trace in my memory. I remember instead the sprawl of her being there, its suddenness, my bed disarranged and the clutter she caused. Also her moods, the work she demanded. It was what I wanted. Ruth brought drugs and showed me how to gum three Rizlas together. We bought cider from the off-licence over the road and got drunk for days at a stretch, then stayed sober for longer. We taught ourselves card games, played board games, did crosswords; I read to her from novels whilst she drew me; sometimes we took our meals on the floor. In the spring we went out on excursions, looking for teashops, museums, places someone's parents might go. I'd brought my mother's old camera from home and presented it to Ruth for her birthday. She arranged her photos in scrapbooks, adding captions cut and pasted from brochures, and called it her work. Then in the summer we dragged my bed to the window, splintering the floorboards, and slept as though in the open, made love in the open, until we noticed one evening a woman in a neighbouring building, ironing and naked, and realised we too were on show, just as exposed. I bought a roller-blind that weekend, and eventually attached it, but still we rarely unfurled it. The bed went back to its alcove.

Over the months Ruth's things began to accumulate in my space, and I didn't much mind them, not whilst she was there. But the moment she'd gone – back to the house she shared with four others – I would gather them up and find somewhere to store them. I took care to fold her clothes neatly – care she wouldn't have taken – and I washed what was dirty. Her bangles and pencils and trinkets filled a box under the bed. She left notes for me too, written on postcards, scraps of cartridge paper, pink notelets, and these I pinned, overlapping, behind the slats of the kitchen partition. Then I could return to myself, to my walls and ceilings and doors. Her absences sometimes lasted for days, sometimes a few hours. I would come home to the surprise of her being there, sitting at the table by the window, taking a bath, thumbing through art books. I would meet her climbing the stairs as I descended. We hardly ever arranged things, when she'd be round or how long she'd remain. In that way we pretended our lives were still separate, and it wasn't until our second year ended, another long summer before us, that I finally met Polly, your grandma.

She had been a few times before, driving down in the morning, gone by mid-afternoon – visits Ruth hadn't mentioned until they were over. You'd loathe her she told me; be grateful I've spared you. She's awful. But Polly, it seemed, was determined to meet me, and when she arrived without warning in that last week of term Ruth was given no choice; her mother insisted. They came round to my flat at midday and Ruth kept her key hidden, knocked three times on my door. I remember the clip of Polly's heels on my floorboards, the sheen of her tights and the bulk of her legs, the powdery scent of her perfume. The bedsprings creaked as she sat down. I had no milk to make tea. I'm sorry, I said, gesturing around me. Not at all, Polly smiled, and glanced at her watch. She said she would take us for lunch, and I suggested the Metropole. Its menu-board, propped up on the pavement outside, was the most expensive we knew. Mum'll hate it, said Ruth. I'm sure it'll be charming, said Polly; and once inside, despite her glances to the bottles in baskets that hung from the walls, and the framed photos of film-stars, and the mould on the wall in our corner, she said again it was charming, though she asked for the flowers on our table to be taken away. A few white petals had fallen. She plucked them from the tablecloth, pink lacquer on her finger-nails, and dropped them in an ashtray. She gave the ashtray to the waitress. Ruth had just begun rolling a cigarette.

It was Polly who determined our seating – she wanted to face me – and guided our choice from the menu, and did most of the talking. I was struck by her hair, a solid mass sculpted back in a wave from the top of her forehead. A single copper-red strand glinted from the shoulder of her blazer. It was gone when she returned from the toilets – the bathroom, she called it – for nothing about her was accidental; her makeup, her jewellery, her clothing, all were immaculate, perfectly matched. Her manners too were impeccable, impenetrable. Subtly she plied me with questions, and I remember her delight, the sudden deepening of her interest, when I mentioned my father. She claimed to know of his work. I felt certain she didn't. How fascinating, she said; you must be very proud of him. Not really, I frowned; no, I don't think so. Well, I'm sure he has every reason to be proud of his son, she smiled, and asked then about my mother – perhaps she too was artistic? I shook my head and refilled my glass. My mother's dead, I said flatly. Polly dabbed her mouth with a napkin, briefly patted my hand. I'm sorry, she said, and looked in annoyance to Ruth. I wasn't aware, she said. I shrugged and said nothing more. Ruth's leg pressed against mine, and for the rest of that meal we listened in silence as Polly recounted in detail the problems she'd had with her builders, the alterations she'd made to her house, the fabrics she'd chosen. She wondered when Ruth would be returning: her bed would need airing. I'm staying in town, Ruth told her; I'm moving to Paul's, we're looking for work. And I nodded, or smiled, though we'd made no such arrangement, hadn't even discussed it. I see, said her mother.

A week later – her own tenancy over – Ruth arrived at my flat with her boxes, her rucksack, and we took jobs in a restaurant called the Atlantis, the sea shifting grey through the windows, clear skies turning to cloud every morning. In the clammy heat of the kitchens I loaded a dishwasher. Ruth waited on tables dressed in clothes she'd last worn to school – a black skirt and black tights, a white blouse and bra – and looking out through my hatch I saw the girl she said her mother always complained of, slow-limbed and sulky, lethargic. The men she served saw something else, and I watched how they teased her, heard later what they'd said to her. Most days she talked about leaving, and when at last she was sacked, the weather worsening, and her attitude, she was told, no better, I dropped my apron in the slops-bin and hurried to join her. She told me to go back; I said that I wouldn't.

We soon found other jobs. Ruth tore tickets in a booth at the funfair; every morning at nine I washed the floors of a nightclub. But we had by then exhausted our pastimes, told all there was to tell about each other, and Ruth no longer drew me; she was tired, she said, of repeating herself. What money I'd saved I spent on a second-hand television, and for the rest of that summer, our evenings enclosed by the rain, we sat up on my bed and watched it. Ruth had said my flat would resemble a prison cell, and living there daily in her company – seeing my walls as she saw them – perhaps this was how it became. We could find no escape from each other there, no escape when we needed one. She called it suffocating, the closeness, and in time we learned how to argue. But that was okay. I had no need of parents, I'd decided – I had no need of anything much – and now I began to believe I had no need of Ruth either. When our course resumed in September she moved herself and her things to another shared house, and we agreed to spend more time apart, though our separations were always short-lived – a few days, a week at the most – and went unnoticed by anyone else. Ruth kept her own key but she no longer wore it. Sometimes she left it behind. What pushed us apart or drew us together was hardly examined, and we rarely spoke of the future. I presumed she would leave me; she would eventually go. I suppose I had always believed that.

SEVEN

The light inside the beach hut was dusty, the air tangible, close with the scent of my aunt. She was Jeannie, my mother's sister, short where my mother was tall, and rounder. She wore a navy blue swimsuit, pinched tight at her waist, wide on her hips, and when she lifted me on to the bench I saw the soft jolt of her breasts and a sudden plump whiteness where the sun wouldn't reach her. I stopped crying and stared. She plucked the snot from my nose with her fingers and dabbed my eyes with a towel. You'll live, she told me. My knee was grazed and gritted with sand. A trickle of blood rolled down my shinbone, and as she cleaned me with water lukewarm from a bottle I gazed at her breasts and said, I wish you weren't just my auntie. Do you? she asked. Who would you like me to be then? My mum, I told her. Jeannie pressed my leg dry with the towel, and quietly said, You already have a mum, Paul. Outside my grandfather coughed; I heard the whirr of the line that tethered my kite to his deck-chair. In the family it was said that my mother had *gone* or *passed on* or *been taken*, though my father had once said *taken herself*. Frowning, I said, No; my mum's dead now. Jeannie spread a finger of Germolene over my wound. She squared it off with her thumb. But she is still your mum, she insisted, not lifting her eyes from her work; and she'll always be that. You only get one. A moth skittered in the slope of the roof and I watched it. It was a year since the funeral, her burial. I hadn't been allowed to attend; and I still hadn't been taken to visit her grave. Why did she die? I asked. She wasn't very well, my aunt said simply, as if the answer was obvious. She peeled the backing from a plaster and stretched it over my knee. But what was wrong with her? I said. Jeannie sighed. I don't know, she replied; I don't think anyone knows that. Not even my mum? Not even your mum, she confirmed, and gripped me under the arms. Her breasts pressed fatly together, the flesh crinkling. Now, she said; finished, and lowered me on to the boards. How's that? I stood lamely beside her, one foot on tiptoe, and looked up to her face. Not even my dad? I persisted; doesn't he know? Jeannie touched the back of my head to guide me outside. I saw the distant seethe of the sea as it broke on the beach, a dog yelping at the waves, and suddenly turned and latched onto her, my arms wrapped tight round her bulk, my face squashed to her belly. She didn't return my embrace but waited, softly breathing, until my hold on her weakened. These are things you'll have to ask your dad, Paul, she said; when you get home. She offered her hand. Okay? she asked, and I nodded. Down on the sand my grandfather was reading his newspaper. He squinted over his glasses as we came out and cleared his throat. All mended? he said. Jeannie lowered herself to a deckchair and patted my arm. Go and play now, she told me.

A week would pass before I saw my father again; several weeks more before I remembered my questions. I was happy on holiday. We were staying in Aunt Jeannie's bungalow, in the coastal town where my mother was born and my grandparents had lived till Grandad's work had brought them inland. Jeannie, being much older, had remained. She was married to a builder called Ian, later to a teacher called Peter, and would always be childless. Every summer until I was fourteen we drove to her home in my grandfather's old car, a black polished Ford Popular with white-walled wheels and red leather seats which he kept, it seemed, solely for those journeys. My father stayed behind with his work, though it was years before I realised there could be no question of his being included, or of wishing to be. Jeannie made up a bed for me in her sewing room, and each August I returned to find the pebbles and shells that I'd collected the previous year, preserved as if I'd not been away, and my crab-lines and sunhats and books, all in their usual places.

There were reminders of myself in other homes too.

During term-time, until I was old enough to fend for myself, it was my father's sister Rene who took me in after school. She fed me and switched on her TV and together we waited for my father to appear in the doorway, red-faced and wearing a trilby, his heavy boots crushing her carpet. And when he wouldn't be coming I stopped overnight, sharing a room with Colin, my cousin, his cot at the foot of my bed, my toys next to his on the floor. At my uncle Ron's, where my father delivered me some weekends, I kept a bicycle in the basement and slept on an old army camp-bed, surrounded by the unwanted clutter of a family of girls. But in my grandparents' house I had a room of my own, my name on a plaque on the door, and there I lived when my father was working away, sometimes also at weekends, often during half-terms. A patch of garden was set aside for my digging. I ran errands for neighbours who remembered my mother, slept beneath her framed photograph, and in my grandparents' bedroom I found a shoebox of snapshots from when she was small, which finally I removed to my own room, but little was said of her, and the photos were never mentioned. When the time came to walk me back home my grandmother would fill her pockets with pennies from a jar in the pantry. She liked to play I Spy and test me with sums, and for each correct answer she subtracted from her pockets and added to mine. At our door she gave me my keys and waited. Her last words were always God bless and she never once came inside.

Our house was very old. It was leased from the college

where my father taught sculpture. Wood beams crossed the ceilings; stone steps led down to the kitchen, up again to the living room. The tourists and students who passed on the pavement darkened our windows, the traffic on the road rattled the latches, but from my room high up at the back I could see out to a river and the vast green expanse of a park called the Racecourse. My father had his studio in the buildings below. He worked from a barn of corrugated fibre and breezeblock, the sliding doors as big as the walls, fluorescent strips hanging on chains from the rafters. A yellow forklift sheltered in a lean-to. His workshop and store cluttered a coach-house, the doors off their hinges, martins and mice in the roof space. I played in a landscape of rusting scrap metal – giant cog wheels and flanges, U-bends and ball-sockets, fat lengths of industrial tubing and thick plates of steel folded like cloth, the rivets like buttons. Whatever the weather at the front of the house, it always seemed cooler behind. The wind whipped through the trees by the river, whined in the pipes and hollows of my father's constructions. Out on the margins lay the work he'd abandoned. A few finished pieces, waxed or whitewashed, rose from the nettles and junk in the sprawl of the courtyard. But closer to the house we had the start of a garden – a trellis on the wall, shrubs and herbs in earthenware pots, bulbs in the window-boxes. I'd helped my mother to plant them.

Often there were people to stay – friends of my father, other artists – and from time to time there were girlfriends, usually younger than he was. A month after my first holiday at Jeannie's he introduced me to Zoë. She came down late to our kitchen one morning, blonde-haired and freckled, her eyes puffy with sleep. She stretched out her arms and yawned. My father stroked her back and she smiled. A few moments later he tipped away the remains of his breakfast and lit up a cigarette. He told Zoë that I would look after her – he had work to do – and as he went out to the yard I felt the cold in the breeze and heard a door slamming upstairs on the draught. Zoë patted her buttocks. Tea, she said brightly, and busied about at the sink, opening drawers and cupboards, finding things, humming. I sat at the table and watched her. There was a rip in the seat of her jeans. Her vest was patterned with daisies. When she sat down she tucked one leg beneath her, tossed her head and pushed back her hair. She poured a mug of weak tea, which she held in both hands. She rested her elbows on the table. Its surface was cracked and uneven, the wood inscribed here and there with the names of our visitors. My father had carved out my own name, with my birthdate beside it; my mother's initials were there next to his. For a short while Zoë gazed down at them, tilting her head, then sipped from her drink and looked up. Is that your kite in the hall? she asked me. I used to love flying kites, she said; when I was a girl. We could take it over the park if you like? It's a nice windy day. She smiled, and I looked to the door. I've got to go now, I told her, and carefully got down from my chair.

But I was bored on my own in my bedroom, and curious,

and when later I smelled cooking I came out to the landing and stood with my face to the banisters. Below in the half-light I could see the balsawood beams of my kite. Slowly I descended the staircase. A pot was simmering on the stove and a fire burned in the grate, but the long wide kitchen was empty. I found Zoë outside in the yard, repotting a few of the plants. She was wearing an oversized jumper that belonged to my father. It's such a shame, she said, standing up; they're desperate for water. The wind flapped in her hair, rustled the leaves on the trellis. Have you come to help me? she said. There was a spillage of soil on the concrete. I gathered it into my hands and solemnly passed it to hers. Thank you, she said, and I backed away to the doorstep. I wiped my hands on my t-shirt and sat down to watch her.

Zoë talked as she worked, describing things from her own childhood, asking questions I didn't reply to, but when she said the shrubs needed pruning I went and fetched her some scissors. I tugged the branches from the bushes as she clipped them. Together we watered the garden. She was making a stew, she told me, and we pinched out some herbs for the saucepan. I followed her into the kitchen and we stood by the fire. Her face was flushed, and when finally she pulled off the jumper I saw there was another beneath it – one my mother had worn. When Zoë removed this she dragged her vest upwards. I glimpsed her breasts then, so small and pale the nipples seemed all of them. She tucked herself into her jeans, but I continued to stare. What is it, Paul? she asked me. Are you going to stay? I demanded. I don't know, she replied; we'll have to see. Then she smiled, and crouched down before me, a hand on each thigh. Would you like me to? she asked. Her eyes were level with mine, unblinking. I shook my head. No, I said firmly, and went to look for my father.

EIGHT

The walk home to my flat would take me six minutes – just time enough to roll up one cigarette and smoke it – and as I leave the college now, a sudden salt wind scouring my face at the corner, I fumble with my tobacco and papers as I often did then, my hands again clumsy, already tight with the cold. I cross towards the chemist's where Ruth bought our contraceptives – the darkened windows grizzled with tinsel, still pasted with ads for suncreams and Kodak – and turn down an alleyway, my shortcut, where I huddle into the wall and cup a hand round my lighter. The flame barely sparks, dies as soon as it catches. When I try again there is nothing, and my feeling, so soon, is to return to our car. You would by now be complaining, wanting to ride on my shoulders.

The passage opens to a terrace of bay-fronted lodgings,

cars parked up on the kerbs, streaks of grit on the pavement, and everything seems smaller, the distances shorter. In a phone booth I see cards for taxis and call-girls, no longer handwritten but printed. On winter nights the traffic round here was constant, slow-moving; women appeared in the glare of the headlamps, slipped back into darkness. Down each of these side-streets there were bedsits, shared houses, people we knew. I trail past bed-and-breakfasts called Spindrift, Ocean Spray, and Trafalgar – my reflection briefly there in the windows, flecks of snow falling, my eyes rheumy with cold – and I remember the couples, older than our parents, sitting out on these patios in summer. Every weekend there'd be suitcases, waiting on door-steps, blocking the pathways. Cabs gleamed in the sunshine; Hoovers droned from the guesthouses. We sometimes drank in the pub on this corner, bought our chips over the road, and thought we belonged here.

My own street begins at the next junction, the buildings much grander, two and three storeys taller. The road slopes lengthily upwards, tree-lined and empty, a belt of brown sludge down its middle. I lived at the end of this first row, directly facing the off-licence. A chalked board on the pavement says, *20% Off Whisky*, and as I walk slowly towards it, fresh snow swirling about me, I toss my lighter aside and turn up my collar. I take out my cough sweets and stand in the doorway and gaze across to my building. It is derelict now. The stuccoed exterior is blistering, daubed ELEC CUT in red paint by the porch. The upper windows are broken, the lower ones boarded, and the door, which I never knew to be locked, is bolted and chained. A tower of scaffolding supports the end wall, a scraggy bush hangs over the guttering, and the joists of my attic are visible now through the gaps in the roof-tiles. The snow, as it thickens, will settle on the floor of my room.

Yet long before I moved out the white of my ceiling was tidemarked with damp. Sudden showers would drip through the plaster. Where once there'd been cracks on the landing, in the end there were rents. I began to find the fissures in my own walls; the tilt in my window-frame, always apparent, came to seem ominous. But when I reported all this to the agency I received no reply. My landlady, I knew – from the builder who worked on our drains – was elderly, a spinster, and senile. I suppose she is dead now. Her property looks as though it has never been lived in.

And I feel nothing, though I would like to, and sense that I ought to. I remember the noises: the pace and weight of Ruth's tread on the stairs, the high screech in her voice when she shouted. I woke to the sound of her coughing in the bathroom, hacking her phlegm in the sink. In summer we caught the muffled boom of the funfair. Her bangles clacked when we made love, the bed rocked and squeaked, and our voices were thick in the darkness. But now there is silence, or not even that. A bus goes by at the top of the hill, somewhere a door slams. I hear a chinking of bottles, muffled footsteps approaching, a cough. But my presence here gives no significance to these things. I left nine years ago, and took with me no more than I'd brought – the rucksack on my back, a plastic bag in each hand. Everything I'd made at the college was discarded; my flat was more bare than I'd found it. Ruth had been gone for three days – our time in this place was over – and I was happy enough then to think I would never return here.

NINE

My father was grinding a sculpture. He stood braced at the knee, the tool tucked close to his groin, and rocked back and forth from the hip. A black rubber cord trailed behind him, flexed as he moved. Sparks shot to the floor in a furious cascade, scattering over the concrete, and the noise was deafening, skirling back from the ceiling. A cigarette burned in the side of his mouth; sweat shone from his forehead. He was wearing goggles and earphones, the straps tufting his hair, and he wasn't aware of me, or seemed not to be. I sat in his chair – an army-surplus fold-out – and slowly swung my legs to and fro. A strip of taut canvas supported my head; my hands were limp on the arm-rests. Sit up, he might say when he saw me, or else point with his thumb to the doors. I knew I wasn't supposed to be there, in the place where he worked.

The sculpture was rusted and covered in chalk marks. Two giant girders rose from a tangle of car parts; a length of undulating steel descended like drapery. In time there would be others just like it, untitled, separately numbered. They stand now in hospital courtyards, shopping precincts, museums. But I was always more interested in the things that surrounded him – in the ladders and gantries and gas cylinders, his chemicals and tools. On a paint tin beside me sat a crocodile clip as big as my hand, and a mug of old coffee, furry with mould. I leaned over and touched the fur with my finger. The grinding wheel spun freely and stopped. The wind was blustering outside. You're here, then? he said, removing his earphones. He pinched the cigarette from his lips and pushed back his goggles. Zoë's making a stew, I told him. Good, he nodded. That's good. He tugged off his gauntlets. In a moment he might tell me to leave. Why did Mum die? I asked him.

But there never would be an answer to that, not from my father, however often I pressed him. We don't talk about it, he'd say; it's happened, it's passed – or else he'd ignore me, as though his mind was elsewhere, as if I'd not spoken. He lit a fresh cigarette now and rummaged about in a toolbox. He found a spanner and removed the wheel from the grinder; he spooled the cord round his arm and hung it over a coat-hook. He examined his sculpture, smoothed a hand where he'd been working, and then brushed some debris into a corner. Finally he nodded. Right, Paul, he said, and lifted me into his arms; let's see about this stew, shall we? He hoisted me on to his shoulders, and as we came from the barn I saw that Zoë was sitting out on our doorstep, hugging herself in the cold. The wind flayed her hair. She didn't smile till we reached her.

She was pretty, I thought. I watched her all through that dinnertime; and later, as she washed up, I fetched my kite from the hall and stood by her side, silently waiting. We went to the park, and I remember the agitated grey of the duck pond, the clouds shredding above us and the flick of her legs as she ran. The kite repeatedly crashed, but when at last it was airborne and the line fully out she crouched behind me, her chin on my shoulder, and passed me the winch. She closed her hands around mine. The kite dipped and rose, looped back on itself, and I looked to her face. She was smiling, the tiniest of gaps between her front teeth. Perhaps I smiled too. She suddenly laughed and attempted to hug me, but the kite fell again, flipped over and plummeted. When it struck the ground it bounced twice and broke. Zoë said she would buy me a new one. I told her I wanted a budgie.

Zoë came often that autumn and winter, though I never knew when to expect her. Some days she worked in the barn with my father, dressed in a pair of his overalls, the sleeves thickly rolled to her elbows. Then in the evenings, as he sat poking the fire and smoking, a bottle of red wine on the hearth, she helped me to build things – monsters from Plasticine, robots from cartons. Once I said, Pretend you're my sister, and she looked to his armchair. What do you think, Dad? she asked him. He shrugged and sipped from his wine, but I could see he was smiling. Some mornings she walked me to school. Most weekends they slept late. I knew I mustn't disturb them. I sat at the top of the stairs and waited, listening for his murmurous voice, her giggling, then crept down to the kitchen. I placed the breakfast bowls and the spoons on the table. Sooner or later they'd join me.

My father had long since moved all his things to our guest-room. In the room he'd vacated my mother's dresses and blouses still hung in the wardrobe, her woollens beneath them. There was a tangle of dry musty tights in a drawer; her shoes were piled in their boxes. The scent that lingered in the cupboards was hers. Over the year and more since her funeral I'd often been in there. I'd dressed in her clothes, played with her makeup. I'd spoken to myself in her mirror. But as the weather worsened that winter – the barn too cold, my father complained, for his work – he packed all these things into a suitcase and repainted the room. He moved the bed to a different wall and lifted the suitcase on to the wardrobe. Eventually I managed to reach it, balancing a stool on a chair, some cushions on top of the stool. The case wasn't locked but the ceiling was low. I raised the lid as far as it would go – a couple of inches – and touched the spikes of her high heels, pulled out her polka-dot headscarf. It didn't occur to me then, nor for years afterwards, that a single case wasn't enough to contain all that there had been.

I kept the scarf under my bed, and added to this her camera, her sunglasses, a wallet of photos. Our house was always untidy, filled with too many things, but I would find little else that belonged to her. My father had already given her jewellery to Aunt Jeannie, her sketchbooks to my grandparents. A few of her paintings, mostly of boats, were stacked in our boxroom, signed McCrory – my grandparents' name – and dated before I was born. But she herself had burned all her papers, the letters and notepads and report cards that she'd kept in her bureau, whilst her paints, she had told me, were too dry to use, her brushes worn out. She had tipped them into the bin and hadn't allowed me to retrieve them. When she'd been angry she'd smashed things – her vases and bowls, the blue-hooped mugs she'd collected, whatever was closest to hand. A photograph of my parents on holiday had gone from its place in the hall. Their wedding album, white-bound and boxed, had disappeared from its shelf in the living room – though this, I felt sure, hadn't happened until Zoë had come.

In my mother's absence I frequently dreamt of her. Sometimes she would be there in our kitchen, searching the cupboards and drawers, unable to find what she wanted, and I would take her upstairs to my bedroom and show her what I'd kept of her things, not merely her scarf but all of her clothes, her jewellery, her papers. Whatever she'd destroyed or discarded was restored; her life had not ended and nothing had changed. She is still your mum, Aunt Jeannie had told me; and she'll always be that. You only get one. And in my games I continued to speak to her. Her face would come to me often, her gestures, the sound of her voice. I pretended she watched as I drew things, or practised my writing, or got myself dressed in the morning. In my imagination she became all patience and sympathy, happier than she had been, and prettier – like Zoë – and when my father shouted at me now, or hit me, I no longer cried for my mother but ran to Zoë instead. And in time it was Zoë that I took to my bedroom. I revealed to her what remained of my mother's belongings; together we looked through her photos. I showed her the suitcase on top of the wardrobe and the paintings of boats in the boxroom. Downstairs I pointed to my mother's place on the sofa, and told Zoë she could sit there now if she wanted. I repeated to her whatever stories I'd heard in my relatives' houses, and made up what I couldn't remember, for Zoë always seemed interested. She asked questions – about my mother, my father, their marriage – far more in the end than I knew how to answer. They just argued, I told her; they shouted.

Zoë and my father didn't have arguments – not like I was used to – but increasingly our meals passed in silence. My father began drinking earlier each day. In the evenings he stared at the television; often he returned to the barn with a bottle. Zoë never went after him, and gave no sign that she'd noticed his leaving. Whatever his mood, she remained cheerful with me. His work, she explained, wasn't going too well, so we mustn't upset him. But it seemed she couldn't find enough things to do, and her visits became shorter, less frequent. My father had no use for her now in his studio. Why waste your time? he shrugged. Why waste yours? she replied; you can't force it. She pressed him to come out with us, and suggested places we might go to. But still he said nothing – he wouldn't be persuaded – and I was glad when Zoë stopped trying. I sensed he was becoming impatient; soon enough he'd get angry.

Then finally, in February, she bought me a budgie. It was there in the kitchen when I came in from school, blue-breasted, white-faced, its wings rippled grey. It sat as if clipped to its perch, a blue dot on each cheek, a red metal ring on its ankle. We stood and admired it. The cage, Zoë told me, had belonged to her grandmother. My father had made the stand that afternoon. He placed an arm round my shoulder, the other round Zoë's, and wondered aloud what we should call it. Mickey, I said, which was my grandfather's name, what his friends called him. Mickey, he confirmed. Then, constricting his voice, he trilled to the bird, *Mickey Michael! Mickey Michael! Mickey Michael!* The budgie didn't move and he started to laugh. Zoë bit her fingernail. She didn't look happy. There had been other gifts – small wooden toys, a kite with long trailing ribbons, and a multicoloured hat that she'd knitted herself – but this, I told her, was my favourite. Good, she said, nodding; I'm glad. Then she turned and went from the room.

A few nights after that I woke to the sound of her crying. I thought for a moment I was hearing my mother, and disorientated, I climbed from the wrong side of my bed. I couldn't find my way to the door and stood still in the darkness. I listened. I'm not *hap*-py! Zoë yelled; I've already *told* you! Her footsteps crossed the landing below me, the bathroom door slammed and she fastened the latch. A little while later my father rattled the handle, whispered her name. He knocked, and called louder, and then he shouted, You are *not*! and forced the door open, I suppose with his shoulder. I got back into bed and burrowed under my blankets. I covered my head with a pillow.

The next morning there were splinters in the door-frame; the bolt-bracket and screws still lay on the floor. I picked them up to give to my father. The only sounds at breakfast came from the budgie, pecking at the bars of its cage, constantly chirping. Zoë collected her bag and said she'd better be going. My father followed her out to the hall; and then Zoë hurried back in to hug me. But none of this was unusual – Zoë, I knew, had her own place to go to – and weeks would pass before I realised she wouldn't be coming again. A pair of her earrings remained in the kitchen. When finally I showed them to my father he nodded. Keep them in your bedroom, he said, and went out to his studio. I hung them in the cage for the budgie to play with.

TEN

I woke from troubling dreams to Ruth's soft tread on the boards, the creak of the wardrobe, her coat-hangers jangling, and rolled on to my belly, as though to embrace her. I raised one knee and stretched out an arm. I breathed her scent in the pillows and felt the warmth she had left there. She laid some clothes on the bed. Her underwear drawer slid open, clunked shut. She parted the curtains. It was a weekday morning, some time after seven, and the sun glared back from the clockface. It shone too from her jewellery, clustered next to the clock, her tangle of earrings and bracelets and chains. Heavy-limbed and lethargic, I tried to remember which day this was, and what chores lay ahead, and as I drifted again into sleep I heard you talking in the room next to ours, your nonsense. I heard the lift in Ruth's voice as she went through to greet you. The first half-hour of your day was always spent in her company, before she went off to work. The rest, until six, would be mine.

You were eighteen months old then, a handful, and constantly mobile, and as I think of you now it seems you ran everywhere, planting your feet as if breaking a fall, tilting, lurching ahead, forever trying to escape me. It seems I spent my days chasing you, and I remember the tantrums – your shattering screams – whenever I caught you. I remember the nights on end when we woke to your wailing, and the days of fretful complaining, your fevers and colds. Often, I know, I was bored, and yet rarely for a moment free of your needs, the work you demanded. There was the long labour of getting you dressed, and the mess that you caused, the smears and spillages and trails of food, the cupboards repeatedly emptied, and the bins and pot-plants upended. I remember the churn of the washing-machine, and the piles of clothes to be ironed, the mop in the hallway, your nappies. Every other task I began was left uncompleted – our walls half stripped of their paper, the ceilings half painted – for nothing much held your interest for long; soon enough I would have to return to you, abandon whatever I'd started. Our house was a shambles, and even when you were sleeping your presence remained – in your buggy and toys and discarded clothes, the scribbles and daubs that I'd pinned to the walls, the crayons I trod on. Everything then seemed to breathe with your energy, whilst I could barely stop yawning.

I remember all this, and my frustration – the fits of complaining to Ruth – and yet I know too that I'd never been happier, more at home in myself. I liked being your father. I was what you'd made me, and often as I looked after you, played my part in your life, I would wonder what you'd later recall of these days, how much would stay with you. It was a time when you lost as much as you learned. A word spoken one day would be forgotten the next; a toy removed from under your nose would hardly be missed. One passing event succeeded another – leaving no mark, it seemed, on your memory – and of course I wanted to preserve it all for you. My camera, permanently cocked on the shelf by the fireplace, had caught the moment you first walked, aged almost one, your arms outstretched in your sleepsuit; and then later, wearing only your nappy, fleeing from Ruth in the garden. It had captured you naked, gazing down at your willy as you peed on the floor of the kitchen, and again as you stood on our bed, blotched all over with spots. There were photographs of you crying, and feeding from Ruth, asleep on her shoulder, and so many more of you smiling. But it is the photographs now I recall, and rarely the moments. One day's traumas were resolved and forgotten; your sudden achievements were soon taken for granted. What remained was the continuing fact of our life together, and of course my camera couldn't capture that.

The albums now are with Ruth, and though I can re-member the sequence of pages, and the notes I pencilled into the margins, what comes to me more often and clearly is waking again that July morning to find you standing beside me, cheerfully babbling, gesticulating, and the momentary pause when you realised I'd woken, the crease in your brow. You gave a sharp squeal, and ran to the end of the bed. You barked something at Ruth and returned. You widened your arms to be lifted. C'mon? you said, nodding; Daddy, c'mon? No, I replied, and rolled into the dip of the mattress, across to my own side of the bed. I heard the pat of your feet as you followed me round, and blearily watched as Ruth slipped out of her nightshirt, pulled it free in one movement. The tea she'd placed on the floor was stewed and lukewarm and it spilled down my chin as I drank. You were tugging my arm, clambering to get onto the bed, and when at last you started to whine I lifted you onto my belly; I held your chest in my broad hands. Your hair was soft and unruly and curled back from your collar. I saw Ruth's blue-green eyes in yours, the dark arch of her eyebrows, her father's cleft in your chin. You were no weight at all, and when I raised you into the air, held you over my head like a trophy, I remember Ruth smiled, her glance meeting mine in the mirror. I remember she zipped up her skirt, turned it round on her hips, and came over to kiss me, as she would every morning, though this time she lingered. She lay down on the bed and nestled against me; she made herself late for work.

ELEVEN

Ruth's home at the start was a barracks three miles from the
coast. Fields of beet grew where once there'd been an airstrip.
The students occupied buildings still painted for camouflage; a
few grey pillboxes watched the horizon. She shared a kitchen
and bathroom with four other girls, caught the same bus in the
mornings, drank with them some evenings, but never felt sure
that they liked her. Half-way through our first term she moved
to a house in the town, and moved again in the second year,
once more in the third. Each time she was invited, for Ruth
always had friends, other people to be with, and wherever we
went – trawling pubs for companions, calling unannounced at
their houses, gatecrashing parties – she always slipped in before
me. And then I would lose her. She wouldn't speak to a crowd,
but withdrew into corners, private conversations like ours, and

sometimes – as I looked on – her eyes would catch mine and she'd frown, as though surprised to find me still there, or disturbed I was watching. I'd sense something then of how it might be when she left me.

But I was happy to watch her. Ruth's hair was fine and very straight and she tucked it repeatedly behind her ears as she listened. When she smiled she became self-conscious, dipping her head as she reached for a glass or her cigarette, allowing her hair to slide forward. Often she sat with one knee drawn to her chin, her arms wrapped tight round her leg, or else eased off her shoes and drew both legs beneath her, almost kneeling, even in pubs, as though curled up on a sofa at home. She made others feel comfortable, and interesting, but always claimed she felt awkward, burdened by what she was told and exposed by what she'd revealed. Walking back to my flat she would cling to my arm and fret about all she had said and not said. Then in my room she'd sit smoking in silence on the edge of the bed, until finally, with a sigh or a groan, she'd stub out her cigarette and come back to me. It was usually then that she'd tell me she loved me. I didn't always want to believe her.

When our time as undergraduates ended there was a party in her house near the college. A short while before it began we sat alone in a pub called the Hurricane, the door wedged open beside us, sunlight glinting from the barrels outside in the yard. Soon most of our friends would be leaving – returning home or travelling abroad, starting jobs, new courses, or moving to

London. One couple was going to get married. Ruth had a place at the Royal College. I'd carried her portfolio down to the interview, and I'd helped to write her application. I hadn't had any plans for myself, and hadn't known what to say when she received her acceptance. The letter now lay on the table before us. I read it again, and folded it neatly, and pushed it back in its envelope. I propped it next to her glass. I really thought you'd be pleased, she said quietly, and I shrugged, then lifted my drink. I am, I replied; it's good. It's just what you wanted, I said.

The lounge was narrow and empty, low-ceilinged, and as I gazed around at the walls, at the red leather benches and stools, polished tables and ashtrays, I thought of waiting rooms, the coach station, and wished all this could be over. I fixed my eyes on a painting near to the bar, a fighter-plane skimming the sea, sandy cliffs in the distance, metallic grey waves. The frame was white, beaded gold, and it hung from a picture rail. It was slightly askew. I angled my head, and knew – from Ruth's silence beside me, her stillness – that she was crying. We ought to get going, I said; but Ruth didn't move. When she turned to face me I looked down at my glass. Have you ever loved me? she asked then; and surprised, I nodded. You've never once said so, she said. From the other room came a murmur of men's voices, the click of the balls on the pool table. I was frightened you'd leave me, I finally told her.

The evening was warm, a scent of blossom and tar in the air, gulls perched on the rooftops. We trailed towards a main road, our steps sluggish, unsteady with drink, and Ruth said, I just thought you'd want to come with me, Paul. I wouldn't have applied otherwise. It doesn't make sense. You can't just go back to your grandma's. You can't go back to all that and spend the rest of your life waiting for the next thing to happen. It's stupid. We're supposed to be an *us*. We paused at a crossing, my hand clammy in hers, and she said, I'm not going to walk out on you, Paul. I'm not. You have to take a chance on that . . . The sun was bright in my eyes, her face indistinct, and I felt the dry blast of a truck as it passed us, breathed the exhaust. I looked down at my feet, the splats of glaze on my boots, the moss dividing the kerbstones. Paul? she said then. What? Say something, she said. I hear you, I murmured, and stepped into the road.

But of course I had not heard her, I was not listening, for always I'd assumed the future would decide itself for me – there would be no choices, no need to act; Ruth would move on and I would not prevent her – and when at last we reached the door to her house we separated, nothing more spoken between us. In each of the rooms there were people, packed boxes, empty bookshelves, and spaces on the wall where once there'd been posters. As I stood amongst the crowd in the kitchen, watching the slow twist of beer from the keg on the table, Ruth reached across me, her hand touching my shoulder, and took away a bottle of wine. When later we crossed on the stairs I smiled, or tried to, and she stroked my arm as she went by, quickly descending. In the press of the hallway we came face to face, and

I turned sideways, her back brushing mine as she edged through. In the living room I watched as she listened to one of our tutors, his arm outstretched to the wall, pinning her in, and I felt sorry for her. Then some time after midnight, making my way to the toilet, I passed her bedroom, heard laughter, several voices, and realised how sorry I felt for myself.

The party had begun in bright sunshine, and as the sky darkened, the pubs emptying and more people arriving, it had spilled out to the garden, on to the flat roof of the kitchen extension and down the front steps to the street. I was by then very drunk, and should have left earlier, but continued to wander from one room to the next, picking up cans where I found them, drinking whatever there was and speaking to no one, until finally, late on in the crush of the kitchen, I found myself standing with Rachel, Ruth's housemate. She smiled when she saw me, a sympathetic crease of her eyes, a tilt of her head, and I guessed they'd been talking. She smelled darkly of perfume, and the mustiness that often also clung to Ruth's clothes. We had to shout into each other's ear. Rachel's hair was thick and long and tickled my face as we talked. I felt the soft pressure of her breast on my arm. She said she didn't like parties, hadn't wanted there to be one. And I told her, Me neither, I don't know why I came, I can't stand anyone here. I slumped back on the wall, bumped into it, and Rachel said something inaudible, her gaze drifting away. I leaned closer, felt myself tipping, falling against her. Rachel gripped me under the arms. What's that? I asked her. Not even Ruth? she said. And frowning, I said, No, Ruth's gone now. I rested my head on her shoulder. She was shorter than Ruth, and much plumper, and I wrapped my arms around her, held on to her softness. The noise of the party receded, everything distant, and I was comfortable then, softly breathing. I closed my eyes, and felt the dark slowly turning, Rachel's legs against mine, her belly, and when at last she eased me away I tried clumsily to kiss her. Perhaps you ought to go home now, she said; and touching her hip, I said, Come with me. Her gaze was steady, appraising. I started to grin, and she smiled. She took hold of my hand and led me out from the kitchen, along the dark hallway. She drew me upstairs. Some girls were descending, and stood aside as we passed. Through the banisters as we climbed I saw into her bedroom, the Indian drapes on her walls, a red lampshade, her mattress. But we wouldn't go in there, already I knew that we wouldn't. She knocked on Ruth's door and let go of my hand. She guided me in. Ruth was sitting alone on the end of her bed. Her face showed no surprise. She tapped some ash into a beercan and swilled it around. She looked down at her feet. Little boy lost, Rachel said, and quietly left us.

TWELVE

The air was damp and still and I could hear a grave being filled, the slice of the shovels. Browned conker cases lay on the ground, last year's brittle leaves. A squirrel skittered through the undergrowth. It leapt on to a headstone, and from there to the trunk of a tree, spiralling upwards. The sky through the branches was vaporous and grey, and from somewhere far off came the sound of a plane, its engine booming, subsiding. I heard the rush of the ring road; I heard Bridget calling my name. She was nearer now than before. I saw the flash of her yellow cagoule, her black shiny hair. In a moment she'd find me. I stood before the grave of Emanuel Cooper and waited. He had died in 1905, aged seventy-eight, whilst Florence May – devoted wife of the above – hadn't fallen asleep until 1918. Reunited, it said.

Paul! Bridget smiled, climbing towards me; I thought I'd lost you. She patted her chest; she was breathless. I'm not lost, I told her. Eleven years old, I passed through the cemetery daily on my way to and from school. I came also at weekends, school holidays, and I remembered the inscriptions – the names and dates of the dead – as effortlessly as I recalled capital cities, chemical formulae, my times tables. I thought I knew every corner. The next stone was crusted with lichens; dark tendrils of ivy crept over it – Cornelius Tuck, whose end was peace, and Elizabeth Tuck, not dead but sleepeth. An angel, green with moss, its features dissolving, rose from a tangle of bushes nearby. Bridget removed the cap from her camera and went closer, adjusting the focus, the aperture. She wore hiking boots, thick socks. She bent her knees and leaned forward. I looked at the spread of her buttocks, and remembered how my father would touch her, standing close by her side in the kitchen. Laughing, she'd push him away with her shoulder. They seemed to be happy together. Where to now? she asked then, cringing as the plane passed above us, its roar like a furnace. I pointed the way.

We had come to visit the bust of Horace John Thirkle, amusement caterer to this city, who had died in 1915. I'd said I knew where to find him. Bridget was Irish, a student at my father's college, his girlfriend, and she was taking pictures of the modern-day Thirkles. Twice a year they erected a fair on the Racecourse at the back of our house. They wintered in caravans on the outskirts of town. Bridget had been there to see them. She had followed their trucks around the county that summer, and some of her photos were going to be shown in a gallery. My own face, pasty-white and determined, appeared at the edge of one frame. A carousel spun in the background, a blur of colour and horses and children. It looked like I was running away, though in fact she had told me to stand there, walk quickly on when she said so.

Horace Thirkle lay close to the top of the rise. I led Bridget past obelisks, shrouded urns, decapitated cherubs, and a plain four-square building in a railed enclosure, the mausoleum of Jeremiah Winter, surgeon and benefactor. The gravestones around us, weathered and tilting, were laid to no obvious grid. Brambles grew wildly, creepers and thistles, and there were beercans too, plastic carrier bags. I saw a pair of soiled underpants, and kicked over a fungus. Bridget wound on a new film as we walked. I hadn't thought she would want to take so many pictures. I was hoping for one more of myself, though I hadn't yet told her. Cautiously I asked, How many's left? and she answered, Thirty-six now, her voice gentle, distracted. She pronounced the thirty as *turty*. I nodded and said, That's him over there, and she gave a sharp sigh. Would you look at that, she said.

The bust was mounted on a plinth of black stone, four pillars around it, a roof like a temple. Twice life-size and bearded, its eyes were dark hollows, gazing out on the streets of the old town, the cathedral spire and the college. I'd seen it too often before. Down to our left was the crematorium chimney. In a few weeks, when the last leaves had fallen, the white regimented rows of the war graves would show through the trees. Half an hour earlier Bridget had paused there, and lingered too at the Garden of Remembrance, then again where the children were buried. She'd watched the paper windmills fitfully stirring, rain-bleached and dirty, and I'd thought she was going to cry, but still she had taken some photos. It was then that I'd left her. And as she peered now through her lens at the bust of Horace John Thirkle I turned and wandered away, clambered up to the old boundary wall. I found the stones of Dear Little Joe, not dead but gone before, and Precious Jemima, only sleeping. There was a woman called Ede Ede, and a man named William Hamlet Denmark. The path was narrow and cobbled and led on to an archway, a black iron gate. On the other side the graves were more recent, and orderly, the grass precincts bisected by roads, dotted with flowers. The gate creaked on its hinges as I went through.

I sat on the rim of a litter bin and zipped up my jacket. I tucked my chin under the collar. Once I had watched from this spot as a coffin was lowered. I was eight or nine then. The people had bowed their heads and leaned into each other. The priest's black cassock had flapped in a breeze. He'd tossed a handful of soil into the grave; and later, as the mourners began to disperse, a woman had stepped forward, holding her hat, and dropped some flowers after it. When the last car had departed – out through the far gates and on to the ring-road – I'd gone down to look. The soil was the colour of sand. The box was a long way below, the flowers obscuring the nameplate, and standing there at the edge I'd thought I was going to fall, tip forward. I'd thought I might jump. My hands were tingling. A green council truck was approaching – rolls of turf on the back, clattering shovels – and for no reason I knew I'd rubbed my eyes and pretended to cry. It wasn't convincing. The workmen, puzzled at first, had finally told me to scat.

I wasn't much good at crying. It wasn't something I did. If my father hit me now – a sudden sharp blow, his hand to the back of my head – I would remain stubbornly upright, and silent. I wouldn't be hurt; or wouldn't allow it to show. At school I was frequently taunted or picked on, and often drawn into fights, always certain of losing, and hardly caring. My motherlessness, it seemed, was a provocation – as was my silence, my stubbornness. I wasn't interested in games, and said very little in class. I got on with my schoolwork: I saw no other reason for being there. You're a solemn wee fella, Bridget once told me, lifting my chin with her finger. Show us your smile, she said. But of course I wouldn't – I refused – though in time, the more often she repeated it, the harder it became to stop myself grinning. Oh no, she'd say then; put it away. Get back in your shell, Paul.

She was calling me now. I got to my feet and stood where

75

she'd see me. One Friday, a few weeks before, I had come this way with a boy called Peter Kelsey, who'd tagged along as I was walking from school. Unsure what he wanted, or why he was being so friendly, I'd shown him the war memorial, I'd shown him where my mother was buried. And he'd seemed interested. Afterwards we had gathered some conkers, filled up our satchels, and when at last I'd got home, the kitchen steamy with cooking, my father had frowned and pointed across to the clock. Late today, Paul, he'd said. I was with someone, I told him. I couldn't say *friend*. I kept that word to myself, clung to it all evening as I threaded my conkers. But the following Monday, in the noise of the playground, I found myself yanked down by my hair. Peter Kelsey walked me round in slow circles. Bent double, one arm raised to cover my face, I twisted my neck and saw a swirl of blazers and ties, the jostling bodies and grins of my classmates. Eventually a teacher had stopped it. Peter Kelsey was breathing hard. I didn't pretend to cry then, but forced out a laugh, dry and defiant. I hurled myself on to him. That was the first time I was placed on detention. I was with a friend, I told my father that evening.

All done, Bridget smiled; they can rest in peace now. Her camera poked out through her cagoule. It was starting to drizzle. She pulled up her hood and slipped a hand under my arm. Lead on, she said, and I took her down the long gravelled track that skirted the new graves, the stones dark and glossy, Cellophane wrap on the flowers, handwritten cards.

Where the cemetery backed on to my school I knew of a skip, mounded with soil and branches, discarded bouquets and ribbons. It was enclosed by high hedges. I supposed it would make a good photo. Is the film finished now? I asked her. Almost, she replied, and I said nothing more. We met a single-lane road, and a sign pointing to the burial chapel, where Bridget turned left, her hand leaving my arm. Isn't it this way? she asked me. I want to show you something, I murmured, and gestured towards a border of shrubs and small trees. There were dedication plaques on the benches. My mother was lying a few yards beyond them.

The grave was tended by my grandparents, and ignored by my father. A plain white block gave her married name and her dates, and like most of the stones in that area it said she had passed away. She was not sleepeth, she was not gone before, and her end was not peace. She wasn't the devoted wife of the above. Ah, Paul, said Bridget, and motioned a sign of the cross. She tucked her hands under her arms. So this is your mum, she said, and I nodded. The noise of the traffic was louder here, the rain coming harder. I rounded my shoulders. I want a picture, I said. A picture? With the camera, I said. Bridget gave a small smile; she gazed at me softly. I'm not sure, Paul, she said; really I'm not. You took all those others, I said. And sighing, reluctant, Bridget flipped the cap from her lens. I did, she admitted; plenty of those. I crouched by the side of the stone. I reached one arm behind it. You swear you won't breathe a word to your dad? she said, and I promised I wouldn't. Then I showed her my smile, my teeth. I held the expression until she was ready, until I heard the doubled click of the shutter. It was the last shot on the film.

THIRTEEN

The Union flags on the promenade are ragged, furiously snapping. Gulls coast above them, stark against the grey sky. The snow dwindles, comes in brief flurries, and even today, in this splitting cold, the seafront cafés and giftshops are open. A few teenagers play the machines in the arcades; the noise along the main stretch is constant. Outside Majestic Amusements there's a mechanical man, his Perspex body full of small toys. He swivels his eyes as I near him. His mouth jolts open, squeaks on its hinges. His name, I remember, is Charlie. *Roll up! Roll up!* his voice crackles. *Roll up for the greatest gifts in town!* I hunch my shoulders, stand a few feet away. My image floats on the window behind him. *Hey! Can you play guitar? My name is Charlie, what's yours?* Euan! you shouted. I'm Euan!

Euan. I drop a pound coin in the slot. A plastic flower-head clunks into the tray, and I take it, though you've had one before; I can sense your disappointment. The flower is fixed to a coil of thin tubing, a black bulb on its end. It squirts water. The picture on the packet shows a clown, his face not unlike Charlie's, and as I turn to leave Charlie calls after me, *Stop! Stop! Don't go away! I'll give you another present today!* But there'll be other days; always at the seaside there are other days. I slip between the parked cars, their windscreens hooded with snow, and hurry over the road. On the beach side it's quieter, seems darker. A jogger lengthens his stride to avoid me. I hear the rasp of his breath and the soft slap of his trainers. There are bird-claws in the snow, his footprints, and I walk in the direction he's come from, past the empty themed spaces, shuttered kiosks and stalls. Overlooking the bowling green there's a red-brick pavilion and a long terrace of benches. In my pocket I have a new lighter, a half-bottle of whisky. I feel for my tobacco, close my fist around it. The benches are too damp to sit on. I shelter in a corner and roll up a cigarette. I break the seal on my bottle and drink to your birthday, and it's then that I see you; another just like you.

The boy is two strides away, standing on the wall that encloses the green. He is five, no older than five, and his arms are stretched wide. He tilts himself left and right, places one foot in front of the other. He is talking to himself. Blue mittens hang limp from his cuffs on lengths of elastic. There's a dark fringe beneath his bobble hat, fat double-knots in his boots. And I am stilled, transfixed. I stand and stare, my bottle in one hand, a fag in the other, and when his mother appears – pushing a smaller child in a buggy – I expect for one moment she'll smile; she will speak and I'll answer. But her face is taut with annoyance, confusion. Her eyes search mine and I cannot look away. She yanks the boy down. She leads him hurriedly out to the road, across towards Charlie, and I continue to stare. Perhaps I ought to call out, run after them. I could offer the flower; I could maybe explain. But this isn't the first time. Like something contagious, I know I'm bad news, best avoided, for even our friends now cross the road to evade me, the telephone no longer rings, and when at last she looks back I shrink into my coat. I swallow from my bottle, and turn, and quickly walk on. The cliffs are there in the distance, our caravan. The flower can take its place in the box by your bunk.

FOURTEEN

I was thirteen when I realised my mother's suitcase of clothes had gone from the top of the wardrobe. For three days we'd had guests, two women from Germany. Katharina had spoken English, though rarely to me; Eva had said very little at all. They were mime artists or dancers, I wasn't quite sure. They'd had their own doorkey and brought home their own food. In the evenings they'd performed at a venue in town, in the mornings they'd slept, and the previous day, returning from school, I'd heard them taking a bath, the water lapping and Katharina reading aloud, Eva suddenly laughing. I'd looked into their room then – a smell like milk souring and the bed disarranged, their clothes on the floor. I was curious about them, vaguely troubled, aroused, and now that they'd gone – a brief note in the kitchen, a bottle of wine for my father – I'd come again to their bedroom, searching for something, I didn't know what. The yellow curtains were closed. In the sandy half-light I peered under the bed. I opened the cupboards and drawers and felt around in the corners. I lifted their pillows and pulled back the blankets. I put my nose to their sheets. All that remained was their smell and I kicked off my shoes and lay face down on the mattress. I had an erection, and when at last I rolled over I saw the empty space near the ceiling.

My father, I knew, would be working, as he had done all through their visit. He hadn't known Katharina and Eva before, and he'd made no effort whilst they were with us. A friend had asked him a favour, he'd said – they'd needed a bed and we had one, so why shouldn't they use it? Because they're ignorant, I'd told him. They're just German, he'd shrugged. And thieves, I thought now, hurrying downstairs and out through the kitchen. He was welding. The vast door to his studio was open, a shuddering blue light in the darkness, a cinematic cast on the walls, his flickering shadow. The smell was pungent as fireworks, the noise snapping and crackling. I shielded my eyes. There were masks on a bench in the corner and I grabbed for the nearest. I covered my face. Urgent, impatient, I stood where I wasn't supposed to. Through my tiny window everything was black but the green point of the weld. The crackling stopped, the light went out. Paul, he said with annoyance, lifting his visor. What is it?

My voice hadn't yet broken, and I heard how I sounded,

high-pitched, excited. They've taken Mum's case, I told him. Who? Those Germans, they've nicked it! Calm down, Paul, he said. A lick of smoke curled from his sculpture. He shook his hands to loosen his gloves, clamped them under his arms to remove them. Which case? he said. Mum's, I repeated; the one with her clothes in. My father picked up a hammer. Oh, that, he said, and chipped some slag from the weld, carried on with his business; that's been gone for a long time. Where? I said; when? Charity, he said simply. But you should've asked me! I protested; why didn't ask you me? Asked you what, Paul? he said, not looking up. If I minded, I said; if I wanted to keep something! He stood and faced me then, his eyes narrowing, the faintest of smiles. Your mother's dresses? he said; I don't think so, son. There might've been something, I insisted. There still is, he replied; there's things all over the house. Take your pick, Paul, he said, waving his hammer; take whatever you like. But that stuff's not hers, I objected; it's just *stuff*, it belongs to the house. My father sighed. So what *do* you want, Paul? Because her case isn't there now, it's gone. And furious, frustrated, I yelled, I want to know why she died! But you won't fucking tell me!

I stepped sharply away, but my father made no motion to hit me. He gave a tired groan and stared for some time at the ceiling. Right, he said finally. Alright, then. He set his mask on the bench and picked up his cigarettes. Come on, he told me, and I followed him, his sagging blue overalls, industrial smell, the worn tread of his boots. He took me into the coach-house. A cat darted past us, carrying something, furtive. Inside the light buzzed and stuttered, flashed on, and for a moment he seemed unsure where to begin, gazed dismally around him, then wheeled a sack-barrow towards the far wall. There was a typist's swivel chair in his way, a stack of wooden pallets, a row of green lockers. He carried the pallets to the door and rolled the chair after them. One by one he tilted the lockers on to the barrow and clanked them aside, revealing a rack of grey metal shelving, a clutter of art-books and boxes and tins – ICI Belco 300, Paripan Dryfast Enamel, Nitromors, Trimite, Holts . . . Breathing heavily, he scratched the back of his neck, flipped the cap from his lighter. He lit a cigarette and stretched out an arm, found what he wanted. Here, he exhaled; take it.

Once, I remembered, my parents' wedding album had slotted into a box, a white cardboard sleeve. The box was gone now, the binding broken. Their names were embossed on the cover – a silver horseshoe, a posy and ribbons – but the padding had been torn round the edges. It was smeared with grease, and the grease was matted with dust. I needed both hands to hold it. My father cleared some things from his workbench and switched on a spot-lamp. He walked away to the door and sat down on the pallets. Go ahead, he said; take a good look. I laid the album on the bench and I opened it carefully. The end-boards were marbled. Thin sheets of paper divided the leaves, opaque and crinkling. The photos were monochrome and I went through them slowly. My father, suited and smiling, was pictured on the path to the church, my uncle Ron at his shoulder, some children behind them and a row of black railings. My mother, ducking, all fabric and flowers, held out a hand to my grandfather as she climbed from the car, a single white shoe on the running board. In a stained-glass enclosure they bowed their heads to the register, the vicar watchful, one hand guiding my mother, her slim fingers and wedding ring. Before the stone arch of the vestibule they posed with linked arms – the splayed white lace of her gown, his dark buttoned suit – at first on their own and then with her parents, his best man, and successively with others, my relatives, strangers, small children, the line gradually lengthening and the camera receding. There were more pictures. In one, I remembered, they'd be kissing; in another, cutting the cake. I'd seen them before. And I didn't go on; I didn't look any further. In every one of the photographs my mother's face was scratched out, scored through to the backing. It seemed she'd used the point of a knife.

She was ill, Paul, my father said then; she hated the sight of herself. She didn't want to be remembered. Do you see what I'm saying? He stood close behind me. I shook my head, and stared down at her, the gouged space where she ought to have been. You should let her rest now, he said; let her go. He reached across me and switched off the lamp. That's what she wanted, he said; she wanted to be forgotten. I was crying, almost, holding it in. You still haven't said how she died, I mumbled. No, son, he said; and I won't. You don't want to know. I do, I told him; I want to know what was wrong with her. No, Paul, he said, and I felt his hand then on my shoulder; I would feel it long after he'd gone. We'll tidy up later, he said.

FIFTEEN

Yesterday I drove forty miles, came to a town which might have been anywhere. I recognised nothing. Life there wouldn't know me. It was late afternoon and darkness had fallen. Silvery lights shone from the trees on the high street. The traffic moved slowly and the pavements were crowded; carrier bags flared in the beam of my headlamps, children's faces, their anoraks. I parked near a church, a crenellated tower of stone, and took a sack of old things from the boot. I cradled it against me, walked in the slush at the side of the road. There was a charity shop near Woolworth's; inside a smell of worn trousers, lavender soap. Two elderly ladies watched from the till. I didn't meet their eyes, and said nothing; I deposited my bag and retreated. But there was no escaping their thanks, their cluttering gratitude. I reached too soon for the door, I had to grab twice. It opened inwards. A pack of Christmas cards fell from a rack, and I stooped red-faced to replace it. Sorry, I said. Outside, empty-handed, I ducked into the shoppers, and wanted to run, but the crowds were too dense, too bulky, and I couldn't make any ground, couldn't push through them. I gave in, and stood still, jostled by so much purpose and motion. I stared down at my feet. I turned and went back to the shop. My bag, still tied, lay next to the counter. Sorry, I said; it's the wrong one. Oh, said the ladies. They stood trimly aside and I made a face of apology, attempted a smile. That one's my son's presents, I explained; I got them mixed up. Oh dear, yes, they said; that's perfectly alright. But the bag was too soft and deflated to contain anything but jumble. I gathered it into my arms and returned to the car. I wedged it against the rear window. It was there in the mirror as I drove home.

I have filled any number of bags. Restless, most days, I drift through the house, opening drawers and scouring the shelves, touching things, holding them – a bowl perhaps, one of your toys – as if in their substance, their weight, I might discover some clue to what's missing. Always something is missing, and yet always there are too many things. I debate in my mind the worth of every item I own. How many spoons do I need, how many towels? Every book, picture and tape, every letter and photo: what was its value before, and what now? All the things I saved and collected, and intended one day to give you, are no longer preserved in the attic but scattered all over the house. I pile what remain of your clothes onto your bed and repeatedly sift through them. I do the same with my own. But I can never be sure what to keep and what to discard. I fill the binbags at random. They sit in every room, and I can hardly remember what's in them.

When I got home I opened a bottle of whisky and closed all the curtains. In the kitchen I stood by the radiator and tried to unknot the bag. But I was shivering, or shaking, and I couldn't undo it. I tore at the plastic, wrenched it apart, and tipped the jumble on to the floor. I got down on my knees. There were so few of your things, and so many of mine, but tangled up with my jumpers and shirts was a sleepsuit, and the shock of seeing it again for a moment unhinged me. I held it to my face and searched for your smell. I tried to picture you wearing it. I looked around for some scissors, a knife. On the chest was a patch in the shape of a heart, and the slogan *Here Comes Love*. I forget now where it came from. It was a hand-me-down; the white cotton was grey from the start. We would never have bought it ourselves – the sentimentality went against what we thought then was our nature – and I never much liked it, only grudgingly used it. It always made me uneasy.

There was a knife in the washing-up bowl. I wiped it clean on a tea-towel and sat at the table. Carefully I unpicked the patch from its stitching, and as I worked I recalled some small thing from last summer – the lacy shadows of trees and Ruth walking beside me, splashes of sun on the pavement. You were riding your bicycle, your feet splayed on the pedals. There was a tea-towel wrapped round your head, a plastic dagger poking from the waist of your shorts. You raced far ahead of us, tunnelling into the distance, and I said, He told me earlier, he's bored being five, he wants to be a teenager. I know, Ruth laughed; it's a shame, and tucked one arm under mine, held on with both hands, her shoulder against me. I lost sight of you then – the pavement curved to the left and you entered the gates of a park. I shouted your name, quickened my pace. He's alright, Ruth said; give him some space, Paul. But of course I could never do that. I tugged my arm free and started to run.

The underside of the patch was adhesive. I tore it away and tossed the sleepsuit back on the pile. I rolled a cigarette and drank from my bottle, the vapour raw on my throat, my sinuses clearing. *Here Comes Love* . . . That night you wore the tea-towel to bed. Long after you'd fallen asleep I came into your room, as I would every evening, holding my breath, listening for yours. I didn't switch on the light but waited for your shape to clear in the darkness. I couldn't breathe until you did. In the gloom then I saw the faintest of movements, the rise of your shoulder, but still I leaned closer. I smelled the sweat in your hair. I peeled the tea-towel from your head and saw your eyes flicker open. You breathed a long sigh, and only then could I leave you.

The patch wouldn't lie flat, the point of the heart curled upwards. I tucked it under my jumper, slipped it into my breast pocket, and slowly I got to my feet. I climbed the stairs to your bedroom and switched on the light. Your bed was stripped bare, the curtains half open. The sleeve of a shirt trailed from a drawer, nothing else in there. Condensation mottled the window, pooled on the ledge. There were rips in the wallpaper where your pictures had been, and a hook in the ceiling for your mobile, some old books and toys on the floor. There was your red-ribboned rosette, your bravery award. A black binbag squatted under your shelves, another on top of the wardrobe. And drunk, determined, I carried these out to the landing. I let them slide down the stairs. I watched as they tumbled, collided, and then I went through to our room. I gathered three bags from there, and collected every other bag in the house, and I dumped them all in the kitchen. I finished my whisky, and unlocked the side door. The cold was sharp in the garden, a taint of soot in the air. A crust of tight snow lay over everything, crunched underfoot. I carried the bags round to the passage and stacked them by the gate for the binmen. I scrawled a note for Ruth and stuck it to the pinboard. And when she visits today, as she said on the phone that she would, she can take whatever else remains in the house, if that's what she wants. She knows now where I've come. The patch is still here in my pocket, and I can't give it away, can't pass it on. It is all that is left to me, all I shall keep, and like the love it is useless.

SIXTEEN

I didn't follow Ruth down to London from college, not straight away. She said she needed a rest from me. She couldn't say for how long – perhaps a few weeks, maybe till Christmas. She would settle into her course, find lodgings, her bearings; and then we would talk. I didn't much mind. Relieved it wasn't the end, I returned to my grandmother's, to the familiar blankness of childhood, and slept again beneath my mother's framed photo, my name on a plaque on the door. Under the bed was my shoebox of snapshots. My school blazer still hung in the wardrobe, the same few pots remained on the window-ledge, but there was little to show for my time as a student – some more photos, my smoking, the graduation scroll that arrived in the post. I had upper second class honours. I took a job in a petrol station, six evenings a week.

Only my grandmother had altered. Tall and thin in my memory, brisk and perpetually busy, she walked now with a stoop, shuffling when she was tired, her legs thickly swollen. The central heating churned for much of the day, the air in the house was stifling, but still she complained of the cold and felt draughts in every room. She rarely went out. A neighbour did much of her shopping; a small man in a cap tended her garden, appeared and left without speaking; and on Tuesdays a woman called Mimi arrived with some magazines, always too busy, it seemed, to take off her coat, though she stayed for an hour and talked without pausing. There were few other visitors: my grandmother said she found them a nuisance. Loosening the ties on her apron, she sat for long periods with her eyes closed – not resting, she told me, but waiting. Her life had gone on for too long and she'd be glad when it ended. I supposed she was missing my grandfather, and eventually I asked her, but she shook her head and denied it, with a force that surprised me. And I hope I shan't be joining him either, she said. Forty-eight years was enough; we were never happy together. I didn't realise, I said. Good, she replied. Then wearily, settling back in her armchair: Good, I'm pleased. You weren't meant to.

But however tired she seemed, my grandmother insisted on doing for me all the things that she'd once done for him; she wouldn't allow me to help her. Breakfast was laid before I woke up, dinner prepared for twelve thirty. We ate together at the kitchen table – the oilcloth faded almost to white – and didn't talk much. My clothes were washed and ironed for Monday and my room smelled always of polish, fresh linen. In the mornings we read our newspapers; in the afternoons we sometimes looked at the television. When I wanted to smoke I went out to the garage.

My grandfather, too, had smoked roll-ups, the same brand as Ruth. I was seventeen when he'd died. He had collapsed in the garage – his workshop – a large wooden shed at the end of the garden. By then he no longer drove; his heart was too bad. The car was tented beneath a tarpaulin, its tyres almost flat. Bits of old bicycle hung from the rafters and walls. Dozens of tobacco tins were labelled for cotter pins, Allen keys, different-sized nails and screws. The tools on his workbench were pitted with rust, the windows too grimy to see through. My grandmother had found him one evening slumped over his vice – he was assembling a bike from spare parts. He used to make them for friends, to give to their grandchildren. He used to make bird-tables, too. There were still several stacked up outside.

At first I thought I might use the shed to make pots, and I cleared some space, then bought a bag of school stoneware from a craft-shop in town, but I took it no further. Instead I lifted one side of the tarpaulin and sat in the car, as I had done when I was small. It smelled of leather and oil, increasingly of ash, and sitting there at the wheel, smoking one cigarette after another, the mileage unchanging, I wrote long letters to Ruth. I couldn't phone her – she said that I mustn't; the calls came through to her landlady's kitchen – but often during the day I would find myself talking to her, whispering under my breath. In my letters I described these conversations in detail, and the gist of my dreams. I kept a tally of my errors at work, daily expecting the sack, and listed my grandmother's sayings and habits, and repeated Mimi's latest news, and reported each visit I made to my father's. I tried to make the letters amusing, I added cartoons, and of course I had no idea how boring Ruth found them, how few she read to the end. Her replies were less frequent, and much shorter.

Then in October, one Sunday, my aunt Jeannie and Peter came over to see us. They sat side by side on the sofa, drinking tea from my grandmother's best china, and talked in raised voices – about the weather, their journey, our distant relations – whilst I listened, content to say nothing, from my grandfather's chair in the corner. My aunt, perfumed and buxom, glanced round at me often. Once she smiled and patted the arm-rest beside her. I stayed where I was. It was Peter's half-term – he was deputy head in a grammar school – and they were driving on later to visit some friends: a former colleague, he said, turning towards me, and his wife. I nodded. The wife was interesting, a teacher of physics but a painter as well. She'd exhibited locally. That's good, I said. Peter thought it a shame that the arts and sciences were usually such strangers, though of course the best science was creative, and many of the arts were grounded in science – ceramics for instance, as I would know. Yes, I said. Aunt Jeannie was watching me. Abruptly she got to her feet. Are these new, Paul? she said, and opened my grandmother's display case.

No, I said, frowning; you've seen them before. Solid-bottomed, as heavy as bricks, there were bits of my pottery all over the house – a few on every window-sill, a dozen or so on the floor of the porch, these two shelves here in the cabinet. At school I had built by hand – laboriously and diligently – crude imitations of the jugs and vases I'd found pictured in books or displayed on the walls of the art room, and which later I would learn to throw in a matter of minutes, though even at college I'd continued to produce little more than imitations, doggedly repeating myself, refining the same few forms to exhaustion, unable to move on until I was told to. And always I had to be told, usually by Ruth. My tutors had seemed to approve of me; technique, for them, was everything.

My aunt removed a cider jar from the cabinet and made a show of its weight, sinking her knees, then replaced it as carefully as a glass figurine. She turned the key in the lock and wiped her hands on her skirt. Well? she asked brightly. Well what? I said. Did you make anything at college, Paul? she said. I bit my lip. I left them behind, I said. She waited. They wouldn't fit in my rucksack, I added. But still she made no response, and finally I said she could look at the photos, though they weren't very interesting. All science and no art, I told Peter. Just go and fetch them, said Jeannie, and reluctantly I climbed the stairs to my bedroom. I opened a window and sat for a while on my bed, smoking a cigarette. I used one of my old pots as an ashtray.

But they're lovely, my aunt told me; aren't they, Peter? Yes, he agreed; very professional. I leant back on the wall and folded my arms. There were snapshots too of my flat, and my tutors, the other students on my course, and any number of Ruth. Jeannie examined these just as intently, and lingered for some time with the last. It had been taken the previous summer. There were freckles on the bridge of Ruth's nose. Jeannie said, She's a nice-looking girl, Paul; and I nodded. Mum? she said; don't you think so? My grandmother's breathing had changed – I thought she was drowsing – but now she opened her eyes and held out an arm. Jeannie passed her the photos. My grandmother set them down in her lap and clasped her hands over them. For some time she said nothing. Peter cleared his throat and suggested he might wait in the car, and I sensed then what was coming. It was time I moved on. I've asked Jeannie to speak to you, my grandmother said.

Later I walked with my aunt to the car. A grey mizzle hung over the street and we paused at the gate. She repeated all she had said, and hoped I wasn't upset. It wasn't that my grandmother didn't want me; and of course I wasn't a burden. But I had my whole life before me. This wasn't where I should be, not any more. Then squeezing my wrist she kissed me, a smell of tea on her breath, her cheeks and neck flushed, and quietly said, You'll think about it anyway? And I said that I would. I watched the car pull away. I turned and walked back to the house. My grandmother hadn't moved from her chair. Her hands were still clasped in her lap, my photos beneath them. Well, Paul, she said, not looking up; I am sorry. That's okay, I said. I was letting the draught in. I'll wash the cups, shall I? No, she told me; I'll do that. Okay, I said, and closed the door quietly between us.

I took my tobacco out to the garage. I tried talking to Ruth, tried composing a letter, but the words were all wrong; I couldn't picture her face, couldn't find the right tone. Instead I looked through my grandfather's drawers and cupboards, the boot of his car, under the seats. But there was nothing to find – nothing I hadn't already seen – and restless, I took down a bike-frame and sized a couple of wheels. I put them together and pumped up the tyres. I cycled out to the end of the street, as far as the shops, and then on past the tower blocks, my school and the graveyard. I had no purpose in mind, and continued along the main road to the old town and the cobbled streets that led to my father's. His door, I knew, wouldn't be locked. The house remained much as it was – inside the same shadows and spaces; familiar objects, furniture, noises – but it wasn't my place, and I knocked rather than let myself in. If he didn't answer, I'd turn and go back – the bike, I'd decided, could do with more work; it had no brakes or mudguards or lights, and only one gear. His footsteps slowly descended the stairs. When he opened the door he nodded, and coughed into his hand, and as I pushed the bike past him he said, One of your grandad's, Paul? Sort of, I answered, and went through to the kitchen. There was a smell of coffee and woodsmoke, clothes drying on the rack by the fire. I sat down at the table and listened for movement upstairs, but the house seemed to be empty.

My father was on a year's sabbatical then, officially a year, though he doubted he'd return to the college. His name, he felt sure, was enough now to sustain him; already most of his work was done to commission; and he'd anyway grown tired of the students, their concepts and notions, pretensions. They had no feel for materials; they had too much to say. He didn't know about Ruth, or her course, the installations and videos she was making. Like my habit of smoking, she was something I kept to myself, kept from him – as he rarely referred to my mother, or the fact that I'd chosen to live with my grandmother. Until that afternoon I'd never once heard him mention my grandad.

He searched the shelves for some cigarettes – there were packets all over the house – and carefully I said, You didn't like him that much, did you? My father gave a short laugh. Mickey? he said. No, Paul, not a lot. He took a light from the cooker and leant back on the worktop. He rubbed at his nose, his stubble, and gazed along the hall to my bike. Still, he said then, I expect your gran'll be missing him; they were together a long while. Not really, I answered; I don't think she liked him much either. No, my father exhaled, tapping his ash on the floor. Your grandad was a bit of a cunt, Paul; he wasn't a very nice man. I felt myself blushing and looked down at the table. I found my name etched into the wood, and I scratched at the varnish, the lines too deep to erase. Then quietly I said, And you weren't, I suppose? My father coughed. He spat in the sink. A cunt? he said. Oh, me too, he agreed; me too. I stared at him. To Mum? I said; or to me? He shrugged and breathed deeply, folded his arms on his chest. Both, he conceded at last; I wasn't much good, I know that. He turned his face to the window – my mother's trellis still there in the yard – and I wondered then if he was waiting, if finally he was ready to answer my questions, whatever I wanted to ask him. But that time, I realised, had gone now. There was nothing more I wanted to know – nothing else I wished to hear from him – and glancing up to the clock I said, I'd better be going, Dad; before it gets dark. My father showed no surprise. He coughed again and stubbed out his cigarette. Okay, Paul, he said; if you're sure. But there's dinner; I could drop you off in the van? I shook my head and pushed back my chair. At the steps to the hall I hesitated. I might be moving to London, I told him. My father looked at me steadily. That's good, Paul, he said, and I nodded, couldn't think what else to say. As I wheeled my bike to the door he drew another cigarette from his packet. He gave a brief wave from the kitchen, and didn't follow me out.

In the evening I dialled Ruth's number. It was her landlady who answered – elderly, Irish, impatient – and said she would fetch her, then shouted her name. Ruth's surprise became silence, a crackle on the line. You still there? I said. Yes, she replied; I'm here. I sat down at the foot of the stairs. How are you? I asked. Fine, she said; okay, I suppose. She took a long breath. What is it, Paul? she said. I stared into the living room, the glass-fronted display case. Upstairs my grandmother was snoring. Nothing really, I said; I just wanted to talk. There's nothing much happening here. My voice was shaking. Ruth didn't speak. I was thinking I might come down, I said; move down, I mean. I see, Ruth said. Is that alright? I asked her. Mm, she said. I pressed the receiver close to my ear. She'd be leaning into a wall, one hand would be cradling her elbow. I tried to imagine her smiling. Ruth? I asked. Sorry, she said; it's a bit awkward right now. To come down? I said. She paused. No, she said; not that. I waited. So how's the course going? I asked. I'll write, Ruth replied; in the morning. Alright, I said. I was shivering. If you're sure. I'd like that; it'd be good. And take care, I said. But the line was already dead.

A few days later a package arrived, a set of three keys

on a cord of brown leather. They're keys, said the card. You don't have to take them, not if you don't want to, but I'd like you to have them ... And then her name, nothing more.

SEVENTEEN

I lost my virginity at fifteen, my window open to the swish of the trees by the river, the factory din of my father at work in his studio. I'd taken a condom from his box in the bathroom, and nervous, I'd kept on my shirt, my socks and my trainers in case I had to dress quickly. My trousers were bunched at my ankles. I felt the cool of the breeze on my legs, the rough weave of the bedspread chafing my knees. Susan lay quiet beneath me, her clothes on the floor, her hands at my shoulders. There was a tightness I hadn't expected, sharp and uncomfortable, and though I tried to go slowly it was over in minutes, a sudden leakage, a sensation of dampness. Have you come? Susan whispered, and I nodded. She stroked the top of my arm. The studio was silent and I listened for footsteps. Perhaps there was something, a scuff on the concrete. I hurried across to the window, hastily belting my trousers, still wearing the condom, and heard a soft snap of elastic, Susan's pants on her hips. The courtyard was empty. The shadows cast by my father's sculptures faded and darkened as the sun passed through the clouds. There were leaf and flower scents in the air, a kite suspended far in the distance, people sitting out on the fields in the park. And smiling, vaguely elated, I fastened the latch on the window. The condom was shrivelled and I pinched it away, made a space in my litter bin. I carefully buried it. Susan buttoned her blouse, flicked her hair loose from the collar. Do you want a cup of tea? I asked then, and she gave a small nod, almost a shrug. If you like, she replied.

I can remember these things, but never quite the sound of her voice. Susan didn't talk much. Our time together passed quietly. Most evenings we sat in my bedroom, or hers – doing our homework, reading, or watching her television – and always when we made love there'd be silence, her hands touching my shoulders, accepting, as remote from me as I was from her. She was very pale, I remember, round-featured, her pallor emphasised by her hair and her eyebrows, which were black and grew thickly. Often she braided her hair, the heavy plait splayed out at the end, sweeping the small of her back. She said I'd once pulled it, in primary school, though I had no memory of that. Susan had always been there, a girl in my class, someone I might pass in the street, and it wasn't until I was fourteen, thirteen perhaps, that I'd noticed her, as most of the other boys had.

She's a well-developed girl, my father had said, the first time I returned from walking her home; big for her age. He seemed to approve, but Susan was regularly taunted in school for her size, for her breasts, and when I think of her now I see the dark crease of her frown and the way she tucked her mouth at the corners, annoyed and defensive. I cannot picture her smiling.

We were together for almost a year, and it was shortly after my sixteenth birthday – old enough now, said one of my cards, to get married, have sex and start smoking – that she told me she thought she was pregnant. Within a few days we would learn that she wasn't – she'd got her dates wrong – and soon after that we'd agree to stop seeing each other. But her tears that first evening had made it seem certain; she was a week overdue and she'd been sick in the night. My dad'll kill me, she said bleakly, sitting up in my bedroom. He'll be livid; he'll make us get married, I just know it. My own father's response, I guessed, would be more scornful, dismissive – the problem would be mine alone to sort out – and wary of approaching him, I skipped school the next morning and caught a bus to see my aunt Rene, his sister, who lived then in a new town some miles from ours.

It wasn't the best time to call. As I came through the door my feet squelched on the carpet. A length of bright copper piping sloped down the staircase, bits of plaster littered the floor, and there was dust in the air, a large hole in the ceiling. My aunt and uncle were shouting upstairs. In the curtained gloom of the living room I found my cousin Colin sprawled out on the sofa, reading a comic. What's going on? I asked him. Nothing, he shrugged. Why aren't you at school? I said. Suspended, he told me, and switched on the television. I sat down in an armchair and waited, and when at last my uncle descended the stairs, still shouting, and slammed the front door behind him, my cousin turned towards me and said, He's got another woman, dirty bastard. He was grinning, and I nodded, attempted a smile. A few moments later I heard Rene's footsteps and followed her through to the kitchen.

It had always been my aunt's manner to talk to me as if I was older, more of a friend than a nephew, and on the long journey over I'd rehearsed in my mind what I would say to her and how she'd respond. We'd be alone in the house, sitting in the quiet of her dining room, and I would admit to having no strong feelings for Susan, secretly to liking other girls more, and she would agree that we'd been foolish, we'd made a mistake, but to get married now would be a worse mistake still. A child, she would say, deserved parents who loved one another, and we were anyway too young, even at sixteen, to take on such a burden, not much more than children ourselves. There'd be concern and sympathy, wry smiles, and finally she would offer to speak to my father, perhaps even arrange to visit Susan's parents. Leave it with me, she would say; I'll see what I can do.

Instead of which she was furious. Her face tight and pale, she began stuffing some bedsheets into the washing-machine, but the bundle was too large, it wouldn't go in, and exasperated she gave up; she turned and suddenly shouted, You *idiot*, Paul! You total bloody idiot, what were you thinking of? I wasn't, I said lamely; it just happened. No, Paul, she snapped; it doesn't just happen, it never just happens – it's the same bloody story, isn't it? It's your mum and dad all over again, the same bloody story. I stared at her, I said nothing, and shaking her head, perhaps realising then what she'd told me, my aunt gestured to the mess in the hallway, to the sheets on the floor, and wearily said, I'm sorry, Paul, it's been a bad day for me, I shouldn't have shouted. What story? I asked her. Never mind, she replied. There isn't a story; I just lost my temper. She plucked at the sleeves of her sweatshirt, rubbed her arms as if she was cold, and then sighed and picked up the kettle. But there wasn't any water – not until her plumber returned – and she called for Colin to come away from the television. She gave him the kettle and sent him next door, and as the gate rattled behind him she quietly said, It was all a long time ago, Paul. I don't see the point in dragging it up now; I think you just ought to leave it. But of course I could never do that. I got from my chair and persisted; I stood where she couldn't ignore me. Is that why they got married, Aunt Rene? Because Mum was pregnant, because she was forced to? No, she said sharply; your mum and dad were in love, Paul; they got married because they wanted to. I shook my head. I don't believe you, I said; I think that's just rubbish, Aunt Rene. I think you're lying. And she glared at me then. She tightened her mouth and pushed past me, flung open the back door. Well, there's the fucking gate, Paul! she shouted, waving her arm. Go and interrogate your father. Better still, ask your bloody grandad. Because it has nothing to do with me, it never bloody did, and I won't be called a liar in my own fucking house! Her face and her arm were shaking. And though I knew that I ought to apologise – and still wanted to talk about Susan – I picked up my jacket and went; I turned for the hallway and left by the front door, slamming it after me.

EIGHTEEN

On the patio outside the Golden Sands Cafeteria there's a fibre-glass ice-cream, two metres tall, and a board saying Leisure Fun Pleasure. A gifts carousel turns in the wind. The white plastic chairs are stacked up in fours, the striped parasols lowered, and a line of plump gulls sits perched on the railings. We often came here as students, and once I took a photo of Ruth standing next to the ice-cream, hunched beneath an umbrella in her fur-hooded parka, sipping tea from a styrofoam cup. That too was December, and later, much later, when we began to visit with you, I tried to take another just like it. I remember the after-noon sun was sharp in your eyes, and the cornet I'd bought you melted on to your hand, then you complained you were seasick. You wouldn't stand still, refused to smile when I asked you, and in the end I gave up; I said we were leaving. But this café, you insisted, was your favourite. A square wooden shack with windows all round, there was the beach below to the right, a small playground behind it. The old man inside sometimes remembered your name. You said you wanted to stay – you wanted to play on the swings – but I was not listening. I walked on ahead, and it was Ruth who promised we would come here again. Maybe tomorrow, she said.

There are no other customers. The old man sits smoking at the table nearest the counter and doesn't glance up as I enter but carefully extinguishes his cigarette and folds over a newspaper. He slowly comes round to serve me, his face netted with wrinkles, deep pouches under his eyes. The food cabinets are empty, the steel surfaces bare. Buckets and spades hang down from the ceiling, beachballs and cricket sets, kites. A fan-heater churns in one corner. My face pricks in the warmth, and when I pull off my hat, my scarf and my gloves, he looks at me briefly, seems for a moment uncertain, then lays out a tray, a saucer and cup, and quietly says, That's tea with no sugar. It isn't a question and he says nothing more. He adds a chocolate bar to the tray and shakes his head at my money, stares away to the door, wiping his hands on his apron. I place some coins by the till. The chocolate, I suppose, would be yours.

I sit facing the beach, the waves breaking grey on the shore, the sands mottled with snow, and hear the click of his lighter behind me. I take out my tobacco, my papers. The vague blur on the horizon is a gas-rig and the sky has no colour. A young family is walking a dog on the strand. They're all wearing wellington boots and the children are searching the tideline. The dog races on, weaves and runs back. My tea is scalding and tasteless. A couple of girls pass by on high clumpy heels, dressed in short skirts, black padded jackets, and I shift in my chair to watch them. They go through to the playground, across a mossy humped bridge, a green narrow stream, and join a group of boys by the swings. One sits drinking a beer, his arms looped round the chains, a sports-bag by his feet. He stands and flexes his arms, scuffs a foot through the snow, then grabs for one of the girls, holds her tight from behind. He tries to lift her, arching his back, and she screams. You were bored being five. You wanted to be a teenager, play out on your own. The old man turns a page of his paper, and I reach again for my tea, but I'm wearing too many layers; my sleeve catches the cup and it topples. I gaze at the spillage, watch it drip to the seat where you ought to be sitting, and then I find I am crying, the tears sudden, surprising. I get to my feet; I don't know what I'm doing. The old man is coming towards me. He lays a cloth over the tea and touches my shoulder. Take your time, son, he says, and gives me a handkerchief. He guides me to a different table, and mops the tea to a bucket, drops the cloth after it. I'll get you a refill, he says. My things remain where I left them. Outside the gifts carousel squeaks as it turns. I hear the dog barking, the teenagers shouting, and I stare at our two empty chairs.

NINETEEN

Christmas Eve, nine years ago, and a gale was blowing. The wind moaned in the chimney, troubled the fire. Rain lashed the windows. Ruth was sitting astride me, drinking a beer, one hand splayed out on my chest. Her face was pink and she wore a pink cardigan. It was a gift from her father that morning – the padded envelope still lay on the carpet, a ball of scrunched wrapping, his card. I'd asked her to wear it. The wool was soft and thin and the sleeves were tight on her arms. A single button was fastened, her breasts loose beneath. I smoothed my hands over it. I think this suits you, I said; it's sexy. You're very sad, Paul, she told me, and lowered herself to her elbows. She dropped the can to the floor. Quietly she said, What've you got me, though? I want to know, Paul. A ring, I said; I'm going to propose to you. She bit my chin. You'd better not, she said. The door rattled; something fell from the scaffolding over the road. I twitched inside her. Are you still cold? I said. I'll light the oven, she murmured, closing her eyes, moving against me. In a minute, she said.

Ruth's flat was a bedsit, a room in a basement – it's a bit of a dungeon, she'd warned me; it's a death-trap, I'd told her – but we were never unhappy down there. A strip of linoleum marked out her kitchen. The cooker and sink backed on to the windows, a fridge in one corner, some shelving above it. The textured paint on her walls was grubby and coarsely applied, the ridges sharp on my arm as I slept, the bed too narrow for two. In the summer, she said, the sun would set behind the buildings that faced us, slant into her room by tea-time. But it was dark all through that winter and we kept the lights on, rarely opened the curtains. The traffic outside was constant. Planes passed overhead, tube-trains beneath us. We felt them coming, a change in the atmosphere, the faintest of rumbles. We heard her landlady, too. She lived on the floor above ours with her son – a man in his fifties, a builder and drinker – and rented the rest of the house. The ceiling creaked with their footsteps, and often they argued. They were bickering now. Ruth sighed. She lifted her head.

What's the time? she asked me. Twelve, I said; just gone. The wind blustered and howled. Happy Christmas, she said, and eased herself from me. She slipped out of the bed and crouched by the oven, and as she pressed the ignition – a rapid series of clicks, the gas jets igniting – I gazed at her bottom. She took another beer from the fridge and swayed as she stood, bumped into the sink. Oops, she said, and pulled back the ring, sipped the froth as it spumed. She left the oven door open. The flames were blue and burned softly, suddenly flared. Are you sure that's safe? I asked her. Unless it blows out, she grinned; or we'll be gassed in our sleep. Then remembering, she covered her mouth. She widened her eyes. Sorry, she said, and climbed in beside me. I took the beer from her. She kissed my cheek, my eyebrows, my ear, and whispered again, I'm sorry. I guided her hand to my penis. Her fingers were cold. But it's gone all soft, she complained. You need to inflate it, I said, and pouting, half smiling, she burrowed under the bedclothes, curling around me.

I listened to the rain, the voices upstairs. Cold air poured in through a vent near the ceiling. The door beside us was bolted and shook in its frame. It opened on to a lobby of brickwork and pipes, junction boxes, cables, Ruth's toilet and shower stall. A flight of stone steps led up to her landlady's kitchen and a door to the garden. We weren't allowed to use the front entrance. We came and went by the dark sloping passage at the side of the building. The nearest tube was a quarter-hour walk, and no one we knew lived near us. We would meet them in cafés and parks; pubs, galleries, their flats. It seemed we were always going to meet someone, and often I came late on my own, the directions written out on the palm of my hand, an *A–Z* in my bag and some cakes to pass round. I had a job then in a factory – Uncle Sam's Cake and Cookie Company – from five until eight every evening. Dressed in blue overalls, the top tied round my waist by the sleeves, I scrubbed and scoured the long metal benches and the sinks and the ovens. I scraped and mopped the cake-mix from the floors and emptied the bins into a skip. The women I worked with liked to tease me; I was slower than they were, and sweated far more, though the sweat seemed to make up for my slowness. Women's work! they called from their aisles. In our tea-breaks we sat in a cloakroom, just next to the toilets, and they talked about sex and the uselessness of men and asked questions about Ruth – what she liked and how often she liked it – that I never knew how to answer. They scolded each other for making me blush; they called me *the boy*.

I was nervous in London, never quite sure where I was, how the parts all connected, and on the tube trains too I would blush, as if my newness was obvious. Wherever I went I walked quickly, a ten-pound note folded into my shoe, my cashcard and wallet in separate pockets. I spoke to no one and didn't often look up. It was a relief to arrive, to find Ruth and her friends, their familiar faces, and to feel I was welcome, expected. You're talking a lot, Ruth once told me, touching my hand; you're doing very well. But it wasn't an effort; I liked being in company then, though I liked leaving it more, returning home on the night-bus to our basement.

We called it our home. There was nowhere else. Ruth's

parents had long since divorced and remarried, and both had moved house several times, a succession of entries scored out in her address book. They lived now two hundred miles apart, in towns Ruth hardly knew. A few of her drawings, she said, were framed and displayed in the guest room at Polly's, but there was little else in the house that she recognised, and nothing at all in her father's. It was nearly a year since she'd last seen him. And though she sometimes replied to her mother's brisk letters – another arrived most Mondays, composed on blue headed notepaper and posted first class – she wrote only to thank Jim for the money he sent her, and the gifts she always discarded. Her thanks were cursory, and she didn't include any news. I said I felt sorry for him – it seemed he could never do right; either he was trying too hard, or not hard enough – but Ruth refused to discuss him, and sulked if I pressed her.

There was silence upstairs. A taxi thrummed in the street; someone shouted. The rain had eased off. Ruth knelt on the bed and unbuttoned her cardigan. She shrugged it from her shoulders and peeled the sleeves from her arms. She drank the last of our beer. Your turn now, she said, and lay down on her belly. She lifted her hips and as I slid into her warmth, my hands tucked under her breasts, she murmured, Be careful, her face close to mine. We hadn't any contraceptives; we hadn't left her room for two days. You're sure? I said. Yes, she said, smiling. Then, Maybe, I don't know . . .

From my father, too, there'd been money – five twenty-pound notes at the end of October, another five notes for Christmas. He didn't write letters. His cards were signed with just his initials, his monogram, and I hadn't yet written to thank him. Now and then I would remember my grandmother, and sit down at Ruth's desk, though I struggled each time to fill much more than a page. Her replies were equally brief, her handwriting shaky, and often she repeated what I'd already told her: *I see the weather's been cold; I'm glad to hear you're both keeping well; I hope things have improved for Ruth at her college.* And always she enclosed a few stamps – a strip of four, sometimes ten, as if for my trouble. I passed them to Ruth. Her course, she felt, had been a mistake, and already she was looking elsewhere, circling jobs in the paper, writing off for more details, three and four times a week. She wasn't an artist, she'd decided, and never would be. The other students had more talent and more confidence. She said they were *glamorous*; she was sure that she wasn't.

What do you think? she would ask me, dumping the forms in my lap. Could I do that job? Would you want to live there? But it hardly mattered what answer I gave her for she had no intention of applying, not yet. She was merely wondering, supposing, thinking ahead, and often we speculated on where we might be in another twelve months, another five years, or twenty. Ruth said she wanted to live by the sea. She imagined weatherboard houses on stilts, cliff-top apartments, grey pebbled cottages – even a beach hut, a caravan, somewhere we could drive to at weekends. I said the car would be an old one, with white-walled wheels, red leather seats, and I would have my own studio, earn my living from pots. Ruth saw me in thick woollen jumpers, a child on my shoulders, waves rolling in from the sea – advertising images, pictures from the magazines she bought – but there was always a child, a Euan or a Jessica to start with. She said she didn't mind which. I was sure I wanted a boy.

Ruth's breath came in gasps, her face pressed to the pillows, one arm crooked round her head, a tangle of hair. I pulled from her and thrust along the cleft of her buttocks, her legs between mine, and came in long trembling rills on her back. The air was cold on my forehead. She sighed and collapsed. She giggled. What a waste, she said. I kissed her arm and rolled on to my side. She shifted to the edge of the bed and reached down for her cardigan. Here, she said, and slung it over her shoulder; you can mop it with this. You're not serious? I said. Ruth? No, she conceded; I suppose not, and offered instead a pair of my underpants. I propped myself on my elbow and carefully wiped her. So what have you got me? she asked then. What do you want? I replied, and clambered across her. I turned off the fire, the oven and lights, and hurried back to the bed. Ruth waited. What would you most like to have? I said. She dragged the quilt over us, looped her arms round me, her legs. Oh, you know, she replied in the darkness; we've discussed it. We never imagined a future without one.

TWENTY

My final design project at college was a tea-service, the clay the colour of chocolate, pitted and rough to the touch, and though I'd left it behind I still remembered the dimensions, and the firing specifications, all the problems I'd had, and the ways I'd found round them. The thing in itself did not matter, the twenty-one separate pieces, for I'd learned enough in their making – I supposed I could always repeat them – and when my grandmother had looked through the photos and told me these were her favourite, and what a fool I'd been to discard them, I had promised I would make her some more, a replica set, just as soon as I had my own studio, my own wheel and kiln. Three years later it seemed she'd forgotten.

Her house by then had become too large for her, the stairs too much of an effort, and she'd moved to her own tiny flat in a place called the Larches. A social worker had arranged it. There was a cord in each of her rooms to summon the warden. A cleaner saw to the communal lounge and the corridors, a council workman looked after the gardens, but there were no other staff. It wasn't a Home, she'd said when I phoned her, and apart from the woman next door, who dropped by most mornings to talk, there was no one to bother her. On Saturday evenings she bought a raffle ticket and sat for an hour in the lounge with her neighbours. Someone would play the piano and the warden would open the drinks bar. My grand-mother returned to her rooms when the singing began. It gave her a headache, she said. On Wednesday afternoons she played two rounds of bingo. Mimi continued to visit on Tuesdays; a volunteer from a neighbouring church did most of her shop-ping; and she still had her old phone number, her radio and television. She said she was comfortable. She never would say she was happy.

It was the start of the summer when we went up to see her, and our train was crowded with families, tourists and students, their suitcases and backpacks. I carried the tea-set on my lap, the cardboard box too large for the racks, too heavy for comfort. It rattled for most of the way. That night we would sleep at my father's, in my old attic bedroom, and the following morning we would visit the Larches, then catch another train north. We had booked a week in a cottage in Scotland, in a town by the sea. It was to be our first holiday together, the only one we ever would have as a couple. Ruth was thirteen weeks pregnant by then, and her bump was beginning to show, but if my father noticed the change in her shape he said nothing, as we said nothing to him. We hadn't yet told anyone; and I didn't want him to hear our news first.

Ruth and my father had met once before, the previous autumn, though then we had stayed with my grandmother, Ruth taking my bedroom upstairs whilst I slept on the floor of the dining room, as my grandmother thought proper. We had come for the weekend, and visited the graveyard, and passed a long afternoon in his company. There had been no offer of food but he'd opened two bottles of wine and invited Ruth down to his studio and explained the work he was doing, its antecedents and influences and where he thought it was going. Reluctant to join them, I'd sat on the back doorstep and waited, hearing his voice and her questions, the wind rustling the leaves on the trellis, and when finally he'd shown us out to the door I'd watched as he kissed her, his hand briefly cupping the back of her head, a cigarette clamped in his fingers. Afterwards, walking back through the old town, Ruth had called him a charmer. He was flirting, I'd said. I know, she'd replied. He isn't really like that, I'd said; he's nothing like that at all. And, touching my arm, she'd said she was teasing – she thought his charm was transparent; she'd found him suffocating, relentless, a bore. Is that better? she'd asked, and I'd nodded. I mean it, she'd added, watching my face; I didn't like him, Paul.

As we stepped now from our train he was waiting at the end of the platform, and he kissed Ruth again, though this time she turned her mouth from him, meeting his lips with her cheek. He grinned and led us out through the gates to the car-park, his hand guiding her arm, and as we drove in his van from the station it was Ruth alone that he talked to. The house was just as untidy, dim-lit and musty, but there were plates on the table, a salad, some pieces of fish on the grill-pan. He smoked as he cooked, and lit up again the moment we'd eaten. The ash lengthened until it dropped to his lap. He swept it away, and carried on talking. He talked for most of that evening, about his work, other artists, the flaws in their thinking. He offered his views on the state of art education, critical theory, public stupidity, and the waste in arts funding. Ruth had a job with a regional arts council; he presumed she'd be interested. And though he coughed repeatedly into his fist as he talked, still he smoked each cigarette back to the filter, then started another. His cough, he said when Ruth mentioned it, was due to the work that he did, the gases and heat, the dust in the atmosphere. Ruth nodded; I didn't bother to argue; and when Ruth too began coughing, I mentioned our journey and said we were tired; I suggested we should go to bed early.

My father yawned and stretched out his arms. He leant back in his chair and gazed at my box on the floor. He linked his fingers over his head and cracked them. So when are we going to see this crockery? he said then. It's for Grandma, I told him.

He looked at me steadily. It was unusual for him to show any interest, either in me or in pottery, anything quite so domestic, but of course there was Ruth – he was different then – and sighing, I lifted the box on to the table; I found a knife and sliced through the Sellotape. My father switched on the lights. He unpacked my work carefully. He placed the bunches of newspaper on the table, as if they too were important, and examined each item in turn, absently stroking his chin, a pair of half-spectacles on the bridge of his nose. And he smiled, smiled at each piece. They were so like real pottery; it seemed to amuse him. I was hoping for a commission to supply Woolworth's, I said. No, no, he muttered, still looking. No, they're better than that, Paul; they have something. They'll do for Grandma, I said. Oh no, he insisted, folding his arms on his chest, the tea-service laid out on the table. It's really not bad, Paul; not bad at all. What do you think, Ruth? he said; is he finally on to something here? And yawning, standing up from the table, she replied, I think Paul's always been on to something. He's better than you think he is. Then she smiled and made her way to the door. Night night, she said.

But whatever my father now thought of my work, the following morning my grandmother shook her head, frowning, and said, You shouldn't have bought it, Paul. No, I can't take it. Her voice was unsteady, and she looked towards Ruth, as if for assistance. I've nowhere to put it, she said. Outside in the gardens an old man was emptying a bag of breadcrumbs on to the lawn. A breeze reversed the leaves on the trees, showed their silvery undersides, and I crouched down on the carpet, began wrapping the plates in their paper. I pressed my mouth to a smile. I don't suppose you have as much room as you used to, I said, and my grandmother agreed, for she'd saved as much of her old furniture and ornaments as she could do, far more than she needed or had space for. The heavy pots in her cabinet were arranged as before. The cups and saucers I'd made on my foundation year, wheel-thrown and clumsy, were again stacked in her kitchen, as if one day she might use them, whilst my earliest pieces, an ashtray, a slab-pot in the shape of a house, still sat by her bed with her pills. Moments after we'd arrived – the door from the dark carpeted corridor unlocked – she'd told us to have a look round. It hadn't taken more than a couple of minutes, and I'd noticed, too, what was missing – the tawny photograph of her wedding day; my grandfather's angling trophies.

Always before my grandmother had accepted whatever I brought her, and she'd never found fault, as my father would do. It was the faults, I supposed, that she'd valued – and this gift was too perfect, too much like real pottery. Of course it must have come from a shop. But still I wanted her to know that I'd made it, and as I packed the last piece in the box I said, Grandma, do you remember the pictures I brought home from college; the ones of my pots? She didn't appear to be listening, but gazed softly at Ruth, as she'd once gazed at her photograph, and again I said, Grandma? Do you remember those photos? Her eyes were filmy, her scalp showing pink through her hair, and she looked at me vaguely. Paul, Ruth said from her chair by the window, her voice a small warning; wasn't there something else you wanted to say? And I nodded. I folded the flaps on the box and pushed it aside. I sat down on the sofa, and smiled to my grandma, and finally I told her our news. Oh, she said as if startled. She clasped one hand in the other, her fingers swollen and waxy, and I noticed then that she no longer wore any rings, the ones my grandfather had given her. It's due in December, I said. Is it? she asked. You're the first person we've told, I added. Am I? she said, and turned again to face Ruth. But you won't want a bastard, dear, will you? No, I suppose not, Ruth replied, and looked over her shoulder, stared out at the gardens. That wouldn't be right, my grandmother said. No. You'll have to get married now, Paul; won't you?

TWENTY-ONE

The steps down from the esplanade are smoothly layered with snow. I descend the boards slowly, holding tight to the handrail. The wind now is ferocious, the beach wide and empty, and soon there'll be darkness. The cold tears at my face, burns in my ears. I hunch into my coat and head out for the strand, my gaze fixed to the ground, searching the pebbles for hagstones, one more to take back to our caravan. The sand is packed hard, solid with ice, and I leave no trace as I walk. The tide is returning. At the rubbish-strewn ridge by the shore-line I hear the waves break and spume on the shingle, the gulls shrieking above me, and for a moment then I glance out, lift my face to the sea, but the cold here is too much, I have to look down. I turn and follow the line of the ridge, scanning the debris, the driftwood and Coke cans, frosted cartons and seaweed, until I find what I've come for.

The stone is shaped like a bird-skull, just small enough for your fist, and the bore-hole is perfect. It's flint, Euan, I say; can you see? I drop it into my pocket and hear the chink of my bottle. I crouch with my back to the sea, the wind searing past me, and pull off my gloves. With numbed fingers I roll up a cigarette. I unbutton my coat and shelter beneath it, catch a flame from my lighter and draw deeply. The coloured bulbs on the esplanade are shining. A concrete ramp slopes down from the last of the beach huts – nearer now than the steps – and I hurry towards it.

The long promenade is empty, as far as the pier behind me, the dark cliffs in the distance. The huts are shuttered and bolted and the paintwork is peeling. At the top of the ramp there's a lifebuoy, and a telephone mounted in a small yellow box. The poster between them says WARNING – THIS COULD BE YOUR CHILD. But the child is a girl. She flops wetly in the arms of a man, her eyes closed, her mouth gaping open. She's no weight at all, and he can't be her father. He regards her face calmly, fixedly, a drip of water on the end of his nose, a quiff of wet hair. His jeans are soaking, his shirt. TEACH WATER SAFETY, it says. Which we did – you had your first badge for swimming, a natural fear of the sea – and as I stare at the girl's limp trailing arm, her damp tendrils of hair, I think only that I ought to phone Ruth, remind her that I've come here. Today at least we should talk. But this phone connects straight to the coastguard – EMERGENCY ONLY – and though I know there's a kiosk fifty yards further back, and another across the wide road, the impulse is already fading. I have nothing to say, and it isn't the sight of this lifeless child that brings me almost to tears but frustration, the dull familiar ache of futility.

Ruth moved out in October, nine weeks ago, and lives now with a friend, a woman called Julie. They used to work in the same building. I don't know how long she'll stay there. Their house is a small one, no different from ours: another long terraced street, cars parked up on both pavements, estate-agent boards in the gardens. Sometimes I drive past it, and once I dialled her number. I listened to Julie, her crackling voice on the answerphone. I heard the beep and said nothing; I replaced the receiver. Our lives were now separate, and though Ruth called me soon after, I let her message run on. She said she would visit – she mentioned your birthday, if that was okay – and I remembered again the moment she'd left me, the pause before she'd opened the door and the silence that remained long after she'd closed it. Her last glance had made no appeal. I made no motion to stop her. There was the creak of the gate and her heels on the pavement, the clunk of her car door. I heard the engine, its slow acceleration, then silence. In the house nothing moved. I stood with arms folded, my head and one shoulder pressed into the wall, my legs crossed at the ankle. I'd always believed she would leave me, she would eventually go. There would be no choices, no need to act. Ruth would move on and I would not prevent her. Minutes passed. I rolled myself from the wall and went through to the living room, sat down in my

135

armchair. The curtains were open and I looked to the window; I met my reflection. An hour or so later I switched off the light and lay down on the sofa.

My cigarette has burnt out. I taste the staleness of ash. A fibre of tobacco has caught in my throat. I bend over and cough, hack hard at the pavement, but nothing will come, I can't shift it, and I think I will vomit. My spittle is sour and thin. My eyes are watering and there are pains in my chest, my temples. I steady myself against the sea-wall and take out my whisky. I swill the taste from my mouth, finish the bottle, and let it drop to the sands. In my pouch there's enough dust for one cigarette, and I ought now to look for an off-licence, take a bus the rest of the way. I'm not sure I can walk any further.

TWENTY-TWO

Two days before Christmas, six years ago. It was dark as evening in mid-afternoon and the house you came home to was freezing. I'd forgotten the heating; I was forgetting a lot of things then. A spray of cards lay on the doormat; a red number five winked from the answerphone. The living room curtains were open. I lit a fire and dragged a chair near it; I fetched some pillows for Ruth to sit down on. She wouldn't take off her coat. You were swaddled inside it, sleeping – your blotched gummy face – and as I stood over you, smiling, one hand on Ruth's shoulder, I looked across to the window to find our reflection and glimpsed a movement outside, someone arriving with flowers, a huge wedge of Cellophane. I hurried out to the porch before the bell could disturb you. Our next-door neigh-bour – we didn't know her name; for almost a year she'd ignored us – brusquely passed them into my arms, and my thanks were effusive. I was floating that day and presumed she had bought them; of course she'd want to share our good fortune. I invited her in; I said she must meet you. But she was already leaving, ducking under the tree by the gate, and seemed not to hear me.

The card said *Many Congratulations, Polly xxx (Mum).* Which is how your grandmother would always sign herself – the *Mum,* the *Grandma,* forever closed off; an afterthought, perhaps an apology. She published an announcement in the *Telegraph* too, then another on each of your birthdays; one more after that. She sent us the clippings. She was good at such things, and could wrap the most awkward of presents. On Father's Day, Mother's Day, New Year and Easter, we knew there'd be gifts – little somethings, she called them – and a letter at the end of each month, her handwriting flawless. She posted a note of condolence when my grandmother died, and a cheque for new clothes when Ruth was promoted, but often too there'd be leaflets – about cot deaths, meningitis, immunisations – and sometimes also an article, neatly clipped from a magazine, offering advice to young parents. One described the resuscitation of small children, another the commonest causes of accidents. We should be wary, it seemed, take nothing for granted; and though Ruth was annoyed, as I was – we'd picked up the same leaflets, read similar articles – still I joined a course in first aid, and eventually passed my exams, for which I also received a card from your grandma. But she very rarely came over to see us, not once you were born. Her life, she complained, was no longer her own – meaning, Ruth said, that *hers* wasn't. Remarried into money, to a former lord mayor, it seemed she spent her days now on charitable works. She sat on several boards of trustees. She was chairwoman of her local hospital's League of Friends. A Sunday magazine profile had called her *redoubtable*, tact and discretion her watchwords. She raised funds for equipment, and organised the activities of two dozen assistants – all dressed in blue pinafores, white blouses – and oversaw the arrangement of the bedside bouquets. She was, said the article, very particular about flowers.

Funereal things, I'd never much liked them, and I'd never bought any for Ruth, but these were different, or I was. They were in most of the first pictures I took, the ones I pinned in my studio, showed to our friends and posted to relatives. Their scent and your sudden presence were equally surprising, elusive. They filled three vases – one next to your cot – and when at last they started to wilt, the petals falling around you, I took a photo to a florist's and came home with another bouquet. It cost more than we could afford, and the selection wasn't quite right, but for almost a year I would continue to refill your vase – though cheaper flowers each time – until your first birthday, when Polly repeated her gesture, the same arrangement exactly. Her message, too, was the same. Ruth shook her head and dropped the card in the bin. She wanted to throw the bouquet away. You can't, I protested. Congratulations for coping so well without me? she replied; because that's what it means, Paul. Sorry you never see me, and sorry I take no interest in Euan, but well done, and here's another bunch of useless bloody flowers . . . And I nodded. I said she needn't go on, but still I insisted on keeping the flowers, though this time when they withered I didn't replace them.

Yet however much Ruth resented your grandmother, it seemed she would always resent your grandfather more. I hadn't met Jim before you were born, though we'd spoken several times on the phone, our conversations far longer than any Ruth would allow him. He worked then for a lingerie company, and travelled most days of the week, a suitcase of samples in the back of his car, a spare suit in a zipper screening one window. A few weeks after your birth he turned up on our doorstep. Small and portly, he brought with him a smell of aftershave, deodorant. His belly domed out over his belt-buckle. His grip when we shook hands was as firm as my father's, and in his stance, his jowly face and deep-clefted chin, the flat bridge of his nose, I thought he looked like a fighter, pugnacious. But he was clearly still nervous of Ruth, her distance, and when she told him you were sleeping he said not to worry, we mustn't disturb you, there were bound to be other days. He said he often passed near us. Oh, just go up, Ruth told him, and walked through to the kitchen. She switched on the kettle. He'll be waking soon anyway, she said; and glancing to me, Jim slipped off his jacket, stepped out of his shoes. They were polished and wrinkled, the same size as Ruth's, and as he climbed the stairs in his socks I saw that his heels were threadbare. At the door to your room he straightened his tie; he hitched up his trousers. It was half an hour before he carried you down. You were sucking on the crook of his finger, gazing up to his face, and when he passed you into Ruth's arms he said, Thank you, then took a step backwards. He's lovely, he said, and fumbled around in his pockets, unfolded a handkerchief. He shook his head at himself and blew his nose loudly. I looked to the floor. Ruth murmured it was time for your feed and eased herself past him. She disappeared to our bedroom.

From my own father, just after New Year, we'd received a bottle of whisky, a single malt in a gold cylindrical box, a year younger than we were. I'd never much liked whisky either, or spirits of any kind, but I'd found a taste for it then. The burn in my throat resembled the parching of smoke, and of course I was no longer a smoker. When that bottle was empty I'd bought a replacement – a supermarket own-brand – and it was this that I opened for Jim as he stood weeping that day in our kitchen. We drank to his grandson, to you, and always then when he called I made sure there was whisky, a glass or two before he departed. And Jim's visits were frequent, as regular as your grandmother's letters. He said he'd be passing our way; he didn't like to impose . . . Sometimes he came at the weekend, and though Ruth never refused him – Euan'll be here, she told him – she hardly spoke whilst he was with us. Often she arranged to go out. It's not me he's coming to see, she argued; I don't see why I have to sit here and watch him. She said she found him embarrassing, the way he fussed over you, the voices he made; and I remember his laugh, the comic-book cackle, each time he lifted you into his arms. He liked to bury his face in your tummy. He pulled off his tie and rolled back his sleeves and got down on the floor with you. It seemed he couldn't hold you enough. His face would be pink when he left, his hair out of order. Your first smile was for Jim, and I thought he deserved it.

Your grandfather's hobby was woodwork and he made almost every present he gave you. The first was a small boat, ten holes in the deck, a numbered peg in each hole. The pegs were painted as sailors, planed smooth and varnished. I tried to slot one into your hand as you sat in his lap, but you dropped it; you gripped my finger instead. Oh well, Ruth said, and picked it up from the floor. She returned the peg to the boat and quietly went from the room. A month or so later he made you a high-chair, which Ruth didn't think would be safe, and then a rocking horse, which she thought you'd fall off. But still he kept trying, though of course Ruth complained he was trying too hard. Once I asked him to make us a bird-table – which he brought the next time, the joints as intricate as any toy that he made – and once, as we sat drinking, talking about tools, his workshop, he showed me his hands. They were like Ruth's, like a woman's, slim-fingered, unblemished. I have to be careful, he said; mustn't chip the nails, not in this business. He gestured out to his car. It's silk, a lot of that stuff. His second marriage had failed and it was his girlfriend, he said, who looked after his hands. He called her his girlfriend. Her name was Liz, and she had three grown-up children, one still at home. She sometimes filed his nails, rubbed cream on his hands, saw to his splinters. He didn't think they'd get married. If the clock works, he shrugged, why mend it? He said these things in confidence, when Ruth was out of the room.

But slowly Ruth thawed, or seemed to. She resigned herself to him, his place in your life, and though she wouldn't invite him to stay overnight, she accepted his lengthening visits, his presence at mealtimes. She came home early from work to meet him. She curled up on our sofa, a whisky glass in her hand, and listened to his stories, asked questions, and drew from him far more about Liz than I could ever tell her. Then one day, as she bent down to lift you, her top buttons undone, Jim glanced at her and said, How big are you now, Ruth? Your bra size? And frowning, she tutted. I'm not telling you, she said. Jim showed us his car-keys, and said he'd be back, and reappeared five minutes later with a box of white knickers and bras. They were seconds, he said, and wouldn't be missed; he also had some in black. Ruth rummaged through them, glanced at the labels. There's a lot of synthetics, she said, and Jim nodded; he waited. They give me a rash, she told him. Her father was sitting on the far side of the room, his hands on his knees. He splayed out his fingers, gazed down at them. He pursed his lips and looked up. And? he said then. They're no good to me, she replied, and closed the flaps on the box, pushed it aside, discarded this gift as she had so many others. I see, said her father.

He said nothing more, and departed soon after, and as his car pulled away Ruth turned towards me and said, Don't bother, Paul; I don't want to hear it. But I wouldn't be silent; for half an hour then we argued, in the hallway, the kitchen, upstairs as I prepared you for bed. So he left your mum, I shouted; who fucking wouldn't? He left *me*! Ruth yelled; he walked out on *me*. He didn't, I told her; he's still around, Ruth; he always has been. He's a millstone, she said; he's pathetic. He's not, I said quietly. He's the only real grandparent Euan's got. And he loves you, I said. Ruth pouted. She sat down on your mattress. You were busying around us, moving your toys from one place to another, and she held out her arms, murmured your name. She tried to lift you on to her lap, but you tugged at her hair, didn't want to be held, and sighing, she let you climb down. She glared for a moment at me. Alright, then! she shouted, and grabbed for a pillow, threw it into the wall. Alright then, she said, and started to cry.

It was two months before we saw your grandfather again, and he said he couldn't stop long, but brought in from his car another selection of knickers and bras. He set the box down at Ruth's feet. One hundred per cent cotton, he said. Or perhaps you'd like silk? There's silk if you want it. Ruth shook her head.

No, she said; these'll be fine. Then, Thank you, she said, and looked out to the street, his car parked next to ours. The boot was still open, his suit in the window. Jim said there wouldn't be any more. His company was folding and he'd have to find a new job. He wouldn't be able to visit so often. Ruth nodded. Euan'll miss you, she said. Then turning to face him, she said, But maybe we could visit you, Dad? Which we did, three or four times a year, and when at last we decided to get married – to make our finances simpler, Ruth told him – Jim and Liz were our witnesses, the only guests we invited.

TWENTY-THREE

My own father was always your *other grandpa*, the one who sent money but never came to our house, who lived far away and was poorly. He's got a bad chest, I told you; he's not very well, and it seemed he required no more explanation than that. On the phone I would hear his labouring breath and the sharp pluck of air as he drew on his cigarettes. Should you still be smoking those? I'd ask him, but of course he wouldn't reply; he wouldn't discuss it. Instead he might ask after Ruth, or change the subject to you. How's the boy doing? he'd say, for it was always *the boy*, and each time I would have to remind him. He's called *Euan*, Dad. Yes, Euan, how's he doing? He's fine, I would tell him, and then describe as much as there was, all I could think of, never quite sure if he was listening, if it was worth going on. Once he confused your birthday with mine, and once he forgot it entirely, but the money was constant, several times every year, and usually cash. We opened a bank account in your name, and sent photos to thank him, later your drawings. We travelled to see him each year in the spring. Yet still he remained as vague about you as you were about him.

Our visits were short – a couple of days at the most – and it was rare even then that he showed much interest in you. He might notice you'd grown, and he always said you were *lively*. But it was only ever Ruth that he wanted to talk to, who held his attention – and of course you couldn't help interrupting, being yourself, until finally I would have to take you outside, sensing Ruth's discomfort, my father's impatience. In the sprawl of his courtyard we would find things to climb on, and places to hide. We'd watch the martins come and go from their nests in the coach-house, and listen for mice, and look for frogs by the river. You would sit behind the wheel of his forklift and pretend you were driving. I'd let you clamber all over his sculptures. But though you often pestered to be allowed inside his studio, the doors would always be padlocked, and it wasn't until our last visit – my father drowsing by the fire, too ill then to object – that I took his keys from the kitchen and said I would show you.

Ruth wandered down with us, hugging herself in the cold. The doors were heavy and loud, as tall as the barn, and wary of waking him, I dragged them just open. I slipped inside and switched on the lights. Everything remained much as it had been, the gas cylinders chained up in pairs, coils of rubber tubing slung from the walls, heaps of scrap-metal piled in the corners. A few bits of sculpture lay around on the concrete, half finished, abandoned, and the benches were cluttered with tools, off-cuts and tins, goggles and earphones. I found a welding mask and tightened the headband. I showed you how the visor flipped up and down. You put it on and tried to walk about in the dark. Be careful, Ruth warned you, and gripped the back of your jumper. You were giggling, pulling away, and for a while I watched you, then sat in my father's old chair, his army-surplus fold-out. On the floor at my side was his bowl, the one he had used as an ashtray, and as I gazed around at his ladders and gantries, the chain-blocks and shelving racks, I remembered how he would smoke as he worked, angling towards his constructions as if hoping to surprise them, a cigarette couched in the palm of his hand, pinched between his forefinger and thumb. Contemplative, he would stand very still, one hand supporting his elbow, the cigarette an inch from his lips. When he was grinding or cutting he would clamp the butt in the side of his mouth. Welding, he'd let it burn out in his bowl. And when at last a piece was completed he would barrel his chest on each inhalation, broadening his shoulders, and smoke each one back to the filter, savouring the last tarry breaths, and slowly exhaling. He'd seem happy enough then to have me around, sitting in his chair, or standing with my back to the vast sliding doors. More often than not he found my presence a nuisance; at least until I was older, until finally I could make myself useful.

He was never ill in my childhood, and it was his smoking, he used to insist, that killed off the germs that gave others their flu, their sniffles. And of course I often had sniffles. At sixteen I would wear a woollen hat in the house to annoy him, sometimes also a scarf. Slouched in front of the television I would lift the neck of my jumper to cover my mouth. I tugged at my sleeves to lengthen them and bunched the cuffs in my fists. I made a point of coughing each time he lit up. And whatever the weather, however warm it became, I rarely left the house without a coat of some kind. I dressed myself from charity shops, the kind of clothes my grandfather would wear – baggy trousers and brown-checked shirts, heavy sweaters and suits, gabardine rain-macs. Susan helped me to choose them; she thought I looked interesting. My father said I looked like one of his students, and it wasn't a compliment, for he was always scornful about the people he taught, even those he used as assistants. He'd find fault with whatever they did; and often they wouldn't return.

It was a few days after I had been to see my aunt Rene that he first asked me to help him. I hadn't yet mentioned my visit, and didn't know how I could, for he was constantly busy it seemed, absorbed in his work, and rarely coming out from his studio. But that afternoon he climbed the stairs to my bedroom and knocked on my door. He said he could use me; it wouldn't take twenty minutes. And I nodded. I was sitting by my radiator, hunched over a book, and with a show of reluctance

I got to my feet; I picked up my scarf. Okay, I shrugged, and as I followed him down, my hands thrust into my pockets, I began to rehearse in my mind what I thought I should say to him. He glanced over his shoulder as we came through the doors. He shook his head at my hat. You won't be needing the tea-cosy, he said, and pointed to a pile of clothes on his chair, the ones he kept for his students. When you're ready, he said, and lit a fresh cigarette. He had wheeled a lifting gantry over his sculpture, and positioned a ladder. His welding gear was prepared, and as I got myself dressed – taking my time – he slowly prowled round his studio, touching things, moving things, restlessly smoking.

His work at that time was enormous, as large as it would ever become. Where once the constructions had appeared self-supporting, the welds just sufficient to prevent them from collapsing, now each separate element – too heavy to be lifted by hand – seemed to float on the last, rising almost as high as the fluorescent strips beneath the rafters. There was as much empty space as there was metal, and the next piece to be welded that day was a ball socket, a few hundredweight of rust-coated steel. A short length of chain was looped through it, the end-links secured to a hook, and from the hook a much longer chain rose through a pulley attached to the gantry. The ball was already suspended ten feet from the ground, and he needed me to hold it steady as he made the first weld, my arms stretched over my head, my face averted from the glare and the sparks. He had made a platform of pallets for me to stand on, and I wore a pair of thick gauntlets – the texture like suede, still moist inside – and some boots with steel toecaps, a hard hat and overalls, my own clothes underneath. How are you doing? he called. And though the pallets were shaky, and my shoulders were aching, I said I was fine.

But my cold that day was genuine, and it was awkward, sweaty work, a confederacy of effort. Afterwards, feverish, I tugged off my scarf and let it fall to the concrete. I sat down, and slowly unbuttoned the overalls, and as my father descended his ladder, breathing heavily, his cheeks and neck flushed, I cleared my throat and cautiously said, I went across to Aunt Rene's last week, Dad. He moved his ladder out of the way, and came to stand by my side, gazing back at his sculpture. For some time he said nothing. Finally he patted my back. It's coming together, he said then; I think it's a good one, Paul. He took out his cigarettes and placed one in his mouth, his lips tight and smiling, then held the pack towards me. I stared at the cigarettes, the clean white ends of the filters. I lifted my chin. His gaze was steady, unflinching, and it seemed clear to me then that he'd already spoken to Rene; obvious too that he wasn't going to discuss it. I don't smoke, I said stiffly, and stepped from the overalls. But you can kill yourself if you want to, I said. I laced up my trainers, and pulled on my wool hat. You're off then, he said. I'm going to Susan's, I told him, and as I began to walk away he tossed my scarf after me. Well don't forget your muffler, he said, and gave his sculpture a firm pat, the noise reverberating like an oil drum.

That same sculpture was still in the yard, the texture of the rust and the welds smoothed away, all the surfaces even. He had painted it yellow – the first time he'd used colour – and though he said he'd had offers, he claimed he couldn't allow it to go. It marked a change; it was important to him. But the base now was encircled by weeds, the paint beginning to flake, and it was the one you most liked to play on. I got up from his chair and went across to the doorway. You came to stand with me, and as I looked out at the sculpture I remembered once taking your photo as you attempted to climb it. I'd asked Ruth to hold you, then noticed my father gazing down from the kitchen. And you, Dad, I'd called, but he'd continued to stare, then shaken his head and retreated indoors. He hadn't approved, and so I'd taken several more, and sent him the duplicates. He kept them in a drawer in the living room, and of all the photos and drawings he'd received the only one on display was a picture of Ruth, her hand on his shoulder. Are we ready? she said to me now, and nodding, I touched her arm and led her across to his bowl. What do you think? I said; I was thinking I might keep it. She pursed her lips and said nothing. In the caravan? I said; or my studio. Don't you think you should wait, Paul? she replied. No, I said; not really. I scattered the ashes and butts in a corner, and looked around for a rag, something to clean it. You've no need of an ashtray anyway, she said. Neither has he, I told her, and wiped it with the leg of some overalls. I took his keys from my pocket and turned off the lights. And this isn't an ashtray, I said; not any more.

TWENTY-FOUR

The sea scared and thrilled you. With my jeans rolled to my knees and my shoes round my neck, I once held your hand at the shore-line. The sand underfoot was smooth and compact, or seemed so. The sun was slowly descending. We watched the waves rolling in, breaking then seeping, thinning towards us. You squealed as the surf licked your toes, danced backwards, and I tightened my grip on your hand; I coaxed you into the water. There was nothing to fear. We submerged ourselves to the ankle. But as the sea pulled away so did the ground, it melted beneath us. We curled our toes, tried to anchor our-selves, but we were tilting, losing our purchase. The glinting backwash raced past us. Your hand slipped from mine as you fell. I tried to help you but you wouldn't allow me. Furious and bawling, you stalked off towards Ruth, the wet seat of your underpants sagging. She widened her arms to embrace you, and as the sea lapped again I started to shiver; I heard the noise you were making, and watched as she led you away.

You always felt safer hiding in the hollows at the base of the cliffs. Red sandstone and chalk, there were tucks and folds there just deep enough for you to crouch down in. We had to pretend we had lost you, pretend surprise when we found you. And our beach, from the start, was a place where we found things. Periwinkles, cowries, mussels, razors, limpets and tellins. We soon learned their names, or I learned them for you. Shells, Ruth called them. Shells, you repeated. I made some earthenware bowls – fat-bellied, wide-rimmed – to keep them in. And another – larger and flatter – for the pebbles with holes in, which were called lucky hagstones and were supposed to be rare, though we found so many we became choosy, kept only the smoothest and tossed the others back to the sand. Above the scalloped ridge of the tideline there were bird-skulls, cuttlefish, bits of driftwood and rope. In the scree that fell from the cliffs we found fossils – spiralling ammonites, bullet-shaped belemnites. And when the tide was low we could search further out, lifting rocks as rounded as turtles and bearded with weed, to find our crustaceans.

You were eight months old the first time we returned to this town. Nothing greatly had changed. Like something outgrown it seemed less than it was. We came for the day, a duty observed, and didn't suppose we would do it again. Alone amongst the seafront cafés and restaurants, the Metropole had closed. We looked in at the windows. The chairs were stacked up on the tables, ghostly white in the darkness. There was a slew of papers and mail on the floor. We ate instead in the Atlantis, and left a large tip for the waitress. We took some photos of the places we knew, and wasted some coins on the amusements. And finally, because we hadn't been there before, and couldn't think what else to do, we pushed and carried you to the top of the cliffs, a mile or so north from the pier. The cafés and gardens slowly dwindled to grey, a strip of bleak concrete, seemingly endless. The drop to the beach grew shorter; the sea wall gave way to sand dunes, marram grass, boardwalks. We turned inland, through a thicket of shade, and emerged to a golf course, where we found a chalk groove in the turf, the start of the cliff-path.

The climb out was a slow one, the air drugged below with bracken and gorse, wide and windy above. There were caravans at the summit, a grid of white dots in a field. You were asleep when we reached them, and we sat for a while in the grass where the land fell away, looking out to the sea, the pale feathered sky. Ruth hitched up her skirt and kicked off her shoes. Dimples formed in her knees when she straightened her legs. She was heavier than she had been. I pillowed my head in her lap and told her I loved her. When you woke you drank from her breast, and later we strolled round the caravans, no two the same and none of them new. We chose our favourite – pale green panels on white, lozenge curves at the corners, a lumber box outside the door. Tufts of grass shivered in the breeze underneath it. I cupped my hands to a window and peered inside, attentive to every detail, trying to imagine. Ruth strapped you into your buggy. She said it was time to get back – her new job began in the morning; we had a long drive – and as we trundled away we passed an old man in a deckchair, the first person we'd seen. How do? he said. Ruth would talk to anyone. A few paces on she touched my arm and told me to wait.

The land, he said, was owned by the council. The ground rent was cheap, but there was no electricity. A gas bottle lasted six weeks. His water came from standpipes and he washed in the shower block. But sooner or later, he said, the site would be plumbed from the main and then the rent would go up. He blamed the EC. He told us the cost of his carpets, his fire surround, and how he'd come by them. They were knocked off, he said, from a holiday camp. He was nobody's fool: he'd bought his caravan from a couple like us, and they'd wanted two thousand, but he'd played one against the other and got it for half. Which was the trouble with marrieds, always divided. He said he was single himself. He would let us know if he heard of anything going – the council kept a waiting list, but he knew of ways round that. Ruth wrote our number in red biro on the racing page of his newspaper. She was sure we could afford it; there was her new salary, and what remained of the money my grandmother had left me. That evening she wrote to the council.

It was two years before the man phoned us. The council, he said, had passed on our names. He didn't remember us. No, I don't recall that, he said. No, that can't be right. He called Ruth *lovey*. He wanted three thousand, and claimed he'd paid almost that ten years before. When we drove out to meet him he showed us his shower stall, his toilet, the new pipes beneath his caravan. He ran the taps at the sink. It was the best thing ever happened, he said; and long overdue – he'd personally been on to the council for years. He mentioned the cost of his carpets, and his fire surround – he'd made a lot of improvements, he said; paid over the odds. We didn't haggle, we agreed to his price. I'd spent the last of my grandmother's money on a new kiln, but Ruth had just been promoted – to Assistant Regional Arts Development Officer – and things were going well for us.

We came out whenever we could, summer and winter – two weeks in July, every bank holiday. Your fifth birthday was spent there, my thirty-first. From inside it always seemed to be raining, always seemed windy, even on the mildest of days. The metal casing pittered as it warmed, then again as it cooled. The slightest movement – Ruth brushing your teeth, drying her hair – sent tremors throughout, as if a gale had suddenly rocked us. The cars that passed on the grey aggregate driveways sounded like hail, or a downpour, and the curtains would tremble. The steady hiss of the mantles at night was soft and continuous. Soon after we'd bought it Ruth said, You'll want it all white; but I said it was fine – the orange swirls in the carpet, the beige and brown benches, pink drapes at the windows, the pale wood veneer. I never wanted to change it. And of course you were happy in our caravan, secure in its dimensions. Every time you glanced up you would find us.

When the sun shone we took our meals outside on a blanket. We played board games, drew pictures, went off on excursions. We descended the rickety steps to the beach. Daily we made a life for ourselves there, consciously made it, and sometimes, as I put you to bed, I'd look over the things you'd collected – the shells shedding grit on your coverlet, the pine-cones and sticks, the brochures and toys – and ask you where they had come from, and which was your favourite. Together we'd assemble the events of your day; I'd help you to place them in order. There were no stories in my childhood, none to speak of, or none that could be spoken. I tried to make sure there were plenty in yours.

But that last evening we spent in the caravan you said you were tired; you wanted to go to bed early. I said I was tired as well. I sat on the edge of your bunk and yawned; I stretched out my arms. There was a bottle of wine in the fridge. In the passage Ruth was getting undressed for her shower. I watched as she stepped from her pants, her breasts swaying, folds creasing her waist as she lifted her legs. There were straps of white on her feet, the ghost of her sandals. When she ducked under the water I stared at her clothes on the floor. I tried to get up, but you twisted out of your sheets and crooked an arm round my neck. I turned my face towards yours, inches between us. You were wearing your new swimming trunks, your red ones. Some girls were drunk and shouting in a neighbouring caravan. Teenagers, you said, and I nodded. I could hear the sea, the distant thump and wail of the fairground. It started to rain. Your eyes were heavy, and I remembered the smell of chlorine when I'd woken that morning, your wet hair on my cheek. The story of that day might have begun there; I sensed you were waiting. What is it? I said, but you didn't reply.

I rested my head against yours and thought back through our day. There was the pub we had gone to that lunchtime. We'd sat by a river in the shade of a lime tree, pestered by midges, the water slow-moving, almost stagnant beside us, and you hadn't wanted to leave, you wouldn't be hurried. In a minute, you'd told us, sipping your drink; I'm busy. Further along was a mill-race, and there I'd held you by the waist and lifted you over the sluice-gates, your screams lost to the roar of the current as it foamed underneath us. Afterwards we'd driven ten miles through villages drowsing in sunshine, looking for a swing-park, and I'd let you sit in the front seat, wearing my sunhat and glasses, Ruth's map spread out on your legs. In the afternoon we'd gone down to the beach, and I'd shown you a crab, semi-translucent, emerging from a melt of wet sludgy sand on my palm, and then we'd dug another trench around Ruth, a speedboat trailing a scar of white spume on the horizon, the sea almost turquoise. In the evening you'd led us along the cliff path into town, swiping with your stick at the bushes, and we'd eaten scampi and chips in a shack called Shrimply the Best, the lights coming out on the pier, the last of the yachts drifting down to the harbour. We'd returned along the tideline at dusk, and it was then that I'd coaxed you into the water, but the slippage had betrayed me, you'd lost your footing and fallen.

There were these things and others – tantrums, arguments, an hour spent cleaning the car – and though I wondered how much you'd recall in five years, or five weeks, still I said nothing. It was time you were sleeping. Ruth had turned off her shower. The rain outside was torrential. The teenagers were laughing. And when at last Ruth stepped from the stall, I kissed your forehead and lifted your sheets; I helped you back into bed. I let that day go. It was the stuff of forgetting, of anyone's holiday, and of course there would be so many others just like it.

TWENTY-FIVE

St Anne's Works is a cluster of reclaimed industrial sheds, an artists' co-operative now, subsidised, grant-funded, a charity. The surrounding streets are derelict, the city centre a ten-minute walk. The sun disappears each afternoon behind a six-storey structure of concrete and glass – the old social security offices, vacant on every floor – whilst across the wide ring-road, strung between two Victorian warehouses, a sagging grey banner advertises *Units to Let*, and always has done, ever since we moved up from London. The traffic never slows. In the pitted, rubble-strewn car-park the only vehicles most days are bicycles, chained to the railings. My studio is one of thirteen conversions in block number five. Plasterboard partitions divide me from my neighbours, and though for a week every summer the studios are open to the public, it is rare that the public takes the trouble to find us. Only the private view generates interest, any kind of attendance – mostly family and friends, and friends of friends, art students, a few local dealers. This summer we hired a jazz band, a bouncy castle, and put up a marquee in the car-park. A city councillor, dressed as though for a wedding, delivered a speech from under the awning, then mimed the cut of a ribbon. I declare the bar open, he said. A few people applauded. Someone with a camera and flashgun took pictures, jotted down names. I crouched by your feet and unbuckled your sandals. What is it? you said. Something, I said; you'll see. I pointed behind you – pointed at nothing – and as you turned to look I grabbed for your waist, scooped up your legs. I ran around the marquee, your jolting weight in my arms, and tipped you on to the castle. Again! you shouted; do it again, Paul. You'd begun calling me Paul. Say *Daddy*, I said; and then I might do.

Later I left you with Ruth and unlocked the door to my studio. I had a four-pack of beer, a float of loose change. Sheets of white catering paper covered the worktops. Hidden beneath were my tools and materials, my buckets and sieves, my father's bowl and your drawings – any evidence of how it might be when I was working, or when you were with me. The benches and shelves, usually so cluttered, were neatly arrayed with the best of the mugs, plates and teapots that I'd failed to sell in previous years, unpacked from their boxes. But though I'd thrown similar things since – marginally better, freer perhaps –

very few of these were displayed. I had other outlets – two galleries in town, a garden centre, the castle museum shop, occasional craft fairs – but I spent less and less time now at my wheel. I produced enough to supply whatever demand there might be, to guarantee some regular income, but I'd become, through you, other than I had been. The forms had changed, my methods. I'd begun building again, slowly by hand, pots like small rocks, like big pebbles, which had gradually grown larger, increasingly unruly, unsuited to anyone's home, I assumed, but our own. I wanted surprises, and mixed glazes and clays with incompatible elements, producing pieces that resembled fossils of bowls, fossils of plates, and I'd stopped removing, smoothing away, any sign of my involvement, the marks and blemishes, the cuts and striations. All of that now remained, the surfaces deep-textured, the glazes cratered and foaming, and a few of those pieces, a dozen perhaps, sat amongst my older work that evening, unpriced and unlisted.

Some people came in, their eyes dutifully scanning the pots as they talked, tapping their ash on my floor. There was a rent reminder from the committee taped to the wall. One elderly man read it in full, peering over the top of his spectacles, then surveyed my work with a frown, and nodded and walked out. A large woman in a blue floral dress picked up each small bowl in turn, examined its base and replaced it. As she came near me I touched her arm and gave her a price-list. Thank you, she said, and laid it on my wheel as she left. It's a shame it's not yellow, someone said then; it'd go well in the bathroom. Do you do them in yellow? her companion asked me. I could do, I shrugged. They stared again at the vase, glanced at each other, and slowly made their way to the door. Others followed, and when at last Ruth brought you in from outside, your face flushed and damp from the bouncing, I was sitting alone, two empty cans under my chair. No sales? she said. None, I replied. Early days yet, she smiled. I took her paper cup and said I'd refill it, I'd be back in a minute.

I thought I wanted a cigarette. It was boredom perhaps, and the beers that I'd drunk, the smoke drifting in from the corridors. Six years and two months had passed since I'd last touched one, my promise to Ruth when she'd found she was pregnant. And it hadn't been difficult – to stop or stay stopped – but just at that moment, released from my studio, I felt I deserved one, a reward for lasting so long. One cigarette on its own would not matter, compared to however many thousands I'd avoided. The thought was exciting and I found myself hurrying; I paid for Ruth's drink with trembling hands and joined a small group of people I knew. Could you spare a fag, John? I said. He carried on speaking, casually passed me his packet and lighter. And the taste, of course, was nothing like I thought I remembered. I began sweating, felt giddy. The air beneath the marquee was stifling. There was a smell of warm canvas, spilled beer, John's leather jacket. People were talking; I heard snatches, their voices, the band playing outside, and I thought I was going to be sick. I let that cigarette burn back to the filter. I dropped it under my foot and ground it into the tarmac. Nicotine, I recalled, was a poison, and I'd proved to myself how little I liked it; I wouldn't be tempted again. I swilled my mouth with Ruth's wine, emptied the cup, and edged away to the bar for another. I went then to the toilets and soaped the smell of the smoke from my fingers.

Ruth was kneeling by my kiln with a dust-pan when at last I returned, sweeping up a smashed vase. The studio was crowded. What happened? I said, and immediately you began blaming the vase. It had hit the back of your hand, you said; it wasn't your fault. Ruth snapped at you; and crying, you wrapped your arms round my legs, complained you wanted to go home. I had no choice but to lift you, and really, I didn't mind, I wanted to go too. Shall we? I asked, but Ruth said there was someone waiting to see me, and glanced past my shoulder. The woman was smiling. Dipping her head, she searched through her bag for a card. It seemed she had a gallery some-where in London, another out on the coast. And so with you in my arms, repeatedly saying you wanted to leave, we talked business, or tried to. I missed so much of what she said. Conscious of the smell of smoke on my breath, I daren't lean any closer. But it was the bigger, rougher pieces that she liked; she wanted to take half a dozen, and commission six more. She pointed them out, and found her chequebook, and said she'd return in a week, collect the remainder some time in September. Right, I said; yes. Okay then, I said, and as she departed Ruth produced my sheet of red stickers. I let you press the dots on the benches. You were careful, precise. You wanted to continue. Perhaps later, I said; we'll see. And by the end of that evening I had sold three more of those pots, and several other things too, including a chocolate-brown tea-set. I sought out the couple with the yellow bathroom and took their address. No obligation to buy, I told them; but I'd phone when it was ready; I could send a photograph, a glaze sample if they would like one. I began work the next day, and everything was ready for collection and parcelling the morning we left for our caravan. It is waiting there still.

I have been back there just once, the last day in October, and I shan't go again. It was a Sunday morning, a damp haze in the air. Church bells were tolling. I went in by the side door. The lights were out and there was no one around. I crept along the dark concrete corridors in silence and enclosed myself in my studio. There were cobwebs, a smell of dry earth. The mildew on the skylight had spread. I sat in my chair and took out my tobacco. I used my father's bowl as an ashtray. The crocks Ruth had collected that evening still lay in the dustpan. Jugs of slip had gone hard and cracked. Dust lay over everything – on the work I'd left out, on my wheel and the floor – but the only footprints were mine. No one else would have gone in there. The same rent reminder was taped to my wall, though I was by then five months in arrears. Like the smoking, I hadn't kept to my commitments. My studio was not in regular use, not in any use at all, which ought to have qualified someone on the waiting list to adopt it. I'd failed to contribute to the running of the co-operative and now owed them thirty hours of my time. I hadn't turned up for the lessons I'd advertised in the newsletter. But of course my circumstances were particularly unusual, extenuating. I should have been served notice to quit. I doubted anyone would ever approach me.

I got up and sat at my wheel. I switched it on – the heavy thrum – and pressed down on the pedal. I leant on my forearms, my hands cupped and ready, six inches apart. I closed my eyes, and remembered. When I first began to learn at the wheel I would work the spinning clay until it collapsed with exhaustion. The splash-tray would be swimming, the floor splattered, my arms and my apron, my neighbours. And the clay, which I could not force to whatever template I had in mind, would lose all substance, its momentum and energy spent. Which was always my failing, to overwork, never trusting to chance, the material. I held to an ideal of perfection like a sickness; and I know, because Ruth told me, that I similarly tried to overwork you. Give him some space, Paul, she'd say; and though in the end I learned to ease off, to let you move on, it worried me now that I'd left it so long. I was always too keen to instruct you. I'd wanted from the start to make of you the perfect imitation of a boy, your childhood exactly proportioned. And I wondered, Did you have time in your five years to grow into yourself, Euan, independent of me, the hands of your father? Those aspects of you I'd found hardest – your obstinacy, energy, refusal – were now what I most valued. You wouldn't be taught, hadn't the patience for lessons. I never could mould you. I hoped I could not. The blue metal disc spun freely, empty. I took my foot from the pedal and pulled the plug from the wall. I gathered up my tobacco and papers, my hat and my gloves. I tugged the rent reminder from my wall. My time in that place was over, and I left the door to the corridor open, my keys in the lock.

TWENTY-SIX

My grandfather coughed and gave the barest of nods. He stepped around me and snorted, spat into the nettles outside in his garden. There was an old tin ashtray on his workbench, a part-smoked cigarette next to his matches. He pinched out the black plug of ash and relit it. So what set this off, Paul? he asked then, up-ending a bicycle. He sat down on a stool, his knees creaking, and adjusted his spectacles. He spun the rear wheel and leaned forward, holding a stub of blue chalk to the rim. Eh? What's behind this? he said. It was early afternoon, a Sunday in April, and my grandmother was cooking. I glanced over my shoulder and saw her blurred form through the steam on the windows. The smells of dinner were thick in my mouth. I just think I should know, I said quietly, as if she might hear us. I'm sixteen, I shrugged; I don't see why I shouldn't be told.

My grandfather nodded – perhaps to the bike, calculating the work to be done – then stopped the wheel spinning. He took the cigarette from his lips and dropped it behind him. And your dad, Paul, he said; what does he have to say? Not a lot, I replied; he won't talk about it, so there's no point in asking. I see, said my grandfather; but you've spoken to your aunt Rene? Yes, I said; sort of. He indicated a tool on the floor. Pass me that up, Paul, he said, and pressed a blunt finger to the air-valve, waited for the tyre to deflate. The tool was a spoke-key. He tucked it beneath his thigh on the stool, his legs wide apart, and plucked one by one at the slim rods, listening for slackness, then tightening the nipples, easing them off. He'd once shown me how to do this, or tried to, but I remembered only his irritation, and the moment he'd snatched the tool from me. He wasn't a patient man, never liked to have to explain things, and as he talked now, his voice sometimes taut with the effort of turning the key, his breath shallow and nasal, I folded my arms and leant back on the doorframe; I kept myself quiet. They were fools, he said, grunting; and I told them so. But I didn't force them into it, not at all, Paul. The wedding was their own decision – white dress, church; nothing to be ashamed of, not as they saw it. She was four months gone by then, four and a half. October the twenty-eighth.

He glanced up and I nodded. There were no dates written down, and of course it wasn't an anniversary my father ever mentioned or celebrated, but returning that day from Aunt

Rene's I'd gone first to the coach-house and retrieved my parents' album of photos. I'd taken it upstairs to my bedroom. Rain had spattered my window. Below in the barn my father was working. Looking down, I'd glimpsed the blue blade of a flame and a sudden bright shower of sparks. A lump of metal had clanked to the floor of his studio and I'd closed my curtains, switched on my desk-lamp. I'd opened the album. In the photographs there was sunshine. The trees in the churchyard were shedding their leaves; dark shadows of branches lay over the pathways, across my father and Ron as they came through the gates. It was autumn, quite clearly, and there could be no doubt that my mother was pregnant. She had chosen her dress for concealment alone. Tucked tight under her bust, everything below was a splay of white fabric; between the accentuation of her breasts and the spread of her hemline she had no shape of her own. I'd examined the faces – my aunt Rene's, Aunt Jeannie's, my other relations' – hoping to find some clue to their thoughts. But there was nothing. They smiled for the camera, held on to their hats, stood as the photographer told them. They posed as they wished to be remembered, and I'd looked instead to the space – gouged from each page – where my mother's own face had been. Flanked by my father and grandfather, the point of her knife had fallen just short of their shoulders, their heads. My grandfather's arms were stiff by his sides, his fists almost clenched, but he too appeared to be smiling.

As he worked methodically now at the wheel, his sleeves rolled high past his elbows, revealing the tattoos on his forearms and the pale ragged skin of his biceps, my grandfather said he hadn't intended to be there; until the eve of the wedding he'd refused to discuss it, the day could happen without him. He remembered my grandmother's coldness – the meals they'd passed without speaking – and Jeannie's persistence, her phone-calls and letters and visits. He remembered, he said, my mother's hysterics. And though he'd regretted it since, in the end he had gone solely to give her away. Just that, Paul, he said; I walked her up the aisle and handed her over. She'd made her choices. I told her she needn't come back after that, not to this house, because she wouldn't be welcome. He shook his head and pushed at the wheel, sat back on his stool. The axle ticked as it turned. That's what I told her, he said, and took off his glasses, stared down at the lenses. For a short while then he was silent. I heard a clatter of pans in the kitchen, the wheeze in his breath, and I waited.

Two years I kept that up, he murmured. I wouldn't entertain her. She used to come when I was at work – whatever shift I was on, she would be round here. Because she was having a hard time of it, Paul. I couldn't ignore that. She needed more help than she got. He folded the spectacles into his pocket and pressed down on his knees, slowly raised himself from the stool. His legs when he stood were bandy and his corduroys hung loosely. He unbuckled his belt and drew the strap a notch tighter. We made our peace anyway, he said; or I'd never have seen you otherwise. You brought us together, you might say. His smile was fleeting. He tugged the lid from a tobacco tin and swiftly rolled up a cigarette, struck a match and inhaled, snapped out the flame. But your dad was a cunt, Paul. I went over there once, confronted him. This was after your mother took bad. Something needed to be said, but there was no getting through to him. He was that wrapped up in himself. He hadn't the time for her – it was always his work. And when he wasn't working he was drinking. Because he liked his booze, son; he was fond of a drink. So was she, I objected. No, my grandfather replied; no, your mum didn't like it. There's the difference, eh? She didn't like it. He moved his stool to one side and lifted the bicycle, hooked it on to the wall. She was drunk when she died, he said then, and looked at me grimly, his face shadowed, unshaven. Killed herself, I said, and my grandfather nodded. Yes, he said. Killed herself, Paul.

Some things, a few, had never been hidden. My mother was nineteen when she married, my father eleven years older. He wasn't at that time a tutor, but a technical assistant, recently graduated himself, for he had left school at fifteen, apprenticed first to a foundry and later employed as a welder. His own father had died in a coal-mine – his mother, he said, of her lungs – and he still kept on the wall in our hallway a painting of some colliery headgears in winter, the paint thickly laid, slabs of white in the foreground, the sky grey and empty. It was one of my mother's, produced when she was a student, but then she had given up college, abandoned her course to get married, and eventually she had given up painting, tipped her brushes and paints in the bin, and burned all her papers. I could remember watching as she'd knelt by the grate, feeding sheet after sheet onto the flames, the pages blackening, curling into themselves, abruptly igniting. I'd knelt with her, and when finally my father had come into the kitchen he'd shouted, and hauled me away, and then they had argued. She had screamed and he'd hit her. Because, I'd supposed, she shouldn't have let me sit so close to the fire, and she shouldn't have been drinking. But of course she was ill. She was often in hospital – four times in one year – and then she had *gone* or *passed on* or *been taken*. She had *taken herself*, my father once said. She gassed herself, my grandfather now told me.

There had been other attempts. Twice before she had used the pills she was taking, her anti-depressants; and once, when she was my age, a mixture of spirits and aspirins. The drinks, he remembered, were left over from Christmas, an inch or so in each bottle – just enough then to make her quite ill, to make her throw up – but he couldn't now recollect what had driven her to it, why she'd become so unhappy. Something and nothing, he said; because it never took much, Paul, not with your mum. It was there in her nature. Jeannie was always the steady one. With Jeannie you knew where you were. But your mum went through extremes, son. She got carried away with herself, and when things didn't work out . . . I took the belt to her once. I thought she'd snap out of it. He gave a shake of his head and took a long breath, then came to stand in the doorway beside me, facing out to the garden, the house, and I smelled the embrocation he used on his knees; I heard my grandmother's voice. Two minutes, she called; you'll be washing your hands? And my grandfather grunted; he drew on his cigarette. I listened to her footsteps receding, the scuff and flap of her slippers, and then quietly I said, But this time she gassed herself, Grandad?

Yes, son, he nodded, and tossed his cigarette into the nettles. Briefly he touched the top of my arm. He stepped into the garden, and as I followed slowly behind him – stooping sometimes to hear what he said – he described how my father had found her, seemingly asleep on the floor of the kitchen, her head in her arms and the oven wide open. It was two in the morning, and she had finished a bottle of whisky. She wasn't long out of hospital. Her doctor had discharged her three days before. She'd been given a course of shock treatment, and it seemed to have helped her. She was a little forgetful perhaps, slow on the uptake, but cheerful. She had said she felt fine, and there wasn't a note; she had left no explanation. Nothing, my grandfather said, and made a noise then like a gasp, something caught in his throat. He paused by the flowers at the end of the lawn, bunched his fists in his pockets, and I glanced to his face, looked quickly away. From the kitchen there was silence. I sensed my grandmother was watching, and cautiously I said,

Maybe I was the reason, Grandad. If she hadn't got pregnant? But my grandfather didn't reply. He had said as much as he could do – as much, I supposed, as there was – and gazing up to my bedroom, the windows blankly reflecting the sky, I remembered the day she had brought me here from our house, the hedges swollen in sunshine and the clack of her heels, the mauve indentation where her ring should have been. In the kitchen she had bent to embrace me and told me to be a good boy; she had said she would come for me later. But of course she hadn't returned – days had passed before I'd seen her again; several weeks more till she'd returned from the hospital – and then again she had gone; she had left me. Because, I'd come to believe, she hadn't wanted a child. She had died because her future was never meant to include me. And as I followed my grandfather now to the kitchen, dipped my hands in the sink and took my place at the table – the blue-painted wall directly before me, my grandparents' chairs to each side – I knew I would probably always believe that.

TWENTY-SEVEN

You hadn't much sense of a future, the shape of a life. I remember your last day at nursery and your first day at school. It was always my job to take and collect you. At first in your buggy, and later walking beside me, we left our house at eight thirty, returned home around four. Your school was called Highfields, and for nearly three years we passed by it routinely, twice daily. Every morning we crossed over the road at the pelican and walked alongside the railings. There were netball hoops in the playground, Portakabins, footballs, a low distant cluster of buildings. The narrow streets all around, deserted before and soon after, would be streaming at that time with children, their parents, and as we eased our way through them, past the noise and crush at the gates and the cars bumping on to the pavements, I would tighten my grip on your hand. But though I knew in the end I would lose you – soon enough you'd take your place inside those railings – it was rare that you showed any interest. Even on your last day of nursery, you didn't look up. The windows glowed in the murk of that morning and I lifted you into my arms; I pointed across to the buildings. That'll be your classroom, I told you; just after Christmas. I *know* that, you said, squirming to get down, pushing against me; you don't have to *show* me, Daddy.

Your nursery was called BusyBees, five long streets further on. The pavements widened and the buildings grew larger. There were basements and forecourts and name-plaques. We passed solicitors, architects, software consultants, an office supplier's, two homes for the elderly. Every day we passed by them. Our route never varied, and we talked very little, at least not to each other. You would speak to yourself, in your own world, and if I heard you say *Daddy* I knew you couldn't mean me. Most mornings you'd have something with you, something from home, and that day it was one of Ruth's compacts. You ambled along at my side, absorbed in your face in the mirror, the click of the clasp and the hinges, and you barely lifted your gaze till we reached the gates of the nursery. Then you dropped it into my pocket, as I knew that you would, for whatever it was you were carrying – a toy or a shell, one of Ruth's things or something of mine – its use for you ended as soon as I pressed on the doorbell, and then you'd be gone, striding past Sophie or Lesley or Hannah, whoever it was that ushered you in, often forgetting to say goodbye in your hurry, your impatience to get on with your day. See you later, I'd call, though that morning I crouched down and hugged you; I kissed the top of your head.

The door wasn't locked when I came to collect you, and the hallway was empty. I paused and breathed deeply. I checked the menu-board for what you'd been eating, and I gazed at your coat-peg, the name sticker fading. I stared at your face in a photograph – two years younger and plumper – and I examined the paintings taped to the walls, any one of which might have been yours. Then for the last time I opened the door to the Quiet Room, where once I would have found you – the smaller children having their story, restlessly listening – and crossed to the noise of the Art Room, where I took my place by the sinks and looked for your head amongst all those others, your dark bob of hair. You were wearing an apron, poster paint on your hands, and when finally you saw me you stopped working abruptly, abandoned the apron and came over to meet me. You tugged at my hand – it was time we were leaving – and though Hannah and Kay came forward to hug you, and I insisted you say goodbye to your friends, and thanks to your teachers, it seemed none of this was important; it meant nothing to you. I collected your toothbrush and mug from the bathroom, and the drawstring bag with your plimsolls, then your workbooks and drawings and paintings, and found you alone in the hallway, trying to button your coat. As I crouched down to help you I smelled the perfume in your clothes, the scent of your teachers. I counted your fingers into your gloves, and eased your hat over your ears; I held you by the shoulders and smiled. And that was the end of it, your three years in that place. You didn't glance back as we left, but rushed on ahead, and when later I asked what you'd been doing all day, you told me you couldn't remember.

In the evening, once she had put you to bed, Ruth sat down on the sofa, curling both legs beneath her, and lifted your workbooks onto her lap. She arranged them in order and tucked back her hair; she licked her thumb and turned the first page. The sheets were dog-eared and stapled, larger than foolscap, and as she browsed through them I went out to the kitchen; I poured myself a drink and came to sit with her. I leant into her shoulder and looked again at your tracings of the preprinted letters and numbers, then your less tidy attempts to write them unaided, with no guidelines to help you. There was your name at the top of each page – a broad scrawl to begin with, becoming tighter and smaller – and your sketches of houses and people, insects and animals, some immediately recognisable, a few only clear from their captions, and all of them strangely proportioned, oddly misshapen. You gave your men fat circles for hands, their fingers as long as their legs. The women had eyes too big for their faces. Well done, Euan, we'd say; that's lovely, no matter what it was that you showed us. And those were the words in my head as I looked at your pictures.

You had done well, applied yourself, approximated a likeness, expressed yourself, and in the process produced something that was lovable, your mark. Ruth was weeping when she put down the last book. I gathered the pile into my arms and said I would take them up to the attic. When? she said sharply. And I paused, laid them back on the floor. Eventually, I smiled; whenever.

Ruth wept too on the morning you started at school; quietly, as she stood in the kitchen, her briefcase packed ready for work. I touched her arm and she sighed, attempted a smile. She shook her head and gathered her things, hurriedly pulled on her coat. She went through to kiss you, and whispered something into your ear, ruffled your hair, but you didn't glance up from the television, and seemed not to notice her leaving. Even as I helped you into your clothes – your green and grey uniform – you didn't take your eyes from the screen. I laced up your shoes, and asked if you wanted to take anything with you, but you laughed and said, No. You chatted excitedly all the way to the school. And though you held my hand tightly as we went through the gates, across the playground and into your classroom, there was no fearfulness or shyness. I remember you stared at a girl who was bawling. You saw a book that you recognised and you showed me. You picked up some sticklebricks. And then you told me to go. You pushed me away, and sat cross-legged on the mat in front of your teacher, patiently, keenly waiting for *what next.* For you there was only ever *what next.* But I didn't go. I went outside and looked back through the window. The other parents edged by me, and I continued to stand there. I waited until your teacher began calling the register, until I saw you lift up your arm, and it was then that I left you, turned and crossed the wide playground. The streets were deserted and I walked slowly home. I had a kiln to unpack that day in my studio, but I went first to your bedroom and collected your workbooks, your scattered drawings and paintings, and took them at last to the attic. I stayed up there all morning, rereading my notebooks, carefully sorting your things. There was so much of it, Euan, and already so much that seemed to be missing.

TWENTY-EIGHT

You were seven months old the first time you sat upright, aged three and three months when at last you abandoned your pushchair. You could write your own name just before you turned four. I know the date you were weaned, and when you caught your first cold; I recorded the moment you took your first steps. I took photos of you feeding from Ruth. None of this, I once thought, should ever be lost or discarded or buried. Whatever you wouldn't remember or notice, I made it my job to preserve. But though your questions now are constant, unceasing, it seems it's only your last day that concerns you, and of course you want to hear every detail. You want to know what we were wearing, and if Ruth smiled for my camera. You want to know the age of the girl, and the name of her dog. You want to know how long it took me to find you, and if you were to blame, and if it's alright to come back now. Again and again, if it's alright to come back now.

That afternoon you were wearing your red swimming trunks, Euan; your new ones, the pair you had slept in. You had worn them all morning under your shorts, and when Ruth helped you undress on the beach I looked to the soft pouch of your penis and saw how grubby you'd made them. She dropped your shorts to the blanket beside her, and then your shirt, your sandals and socks, and later, when I began taking my pictures, I pushed them aside with my foot; I moved them out of the frame. Like me you burned easily, but we'd forgotten your sunblock. I said to Ruth that she ought to leave your shirt on, and I remember the taut globe of your belly – which always surprised me – and the way you placed your hand there as you drank from our bottle. Half an hour only, Ruth told you; then you'll have to cover up again. She touched the top of your arm, where the skin was beginning to flake. Do you hear me? she said, and you nodded. Some water dribbled on to your chin and she wiped it away with her thumb.

Ruth that day was wearing her red cotton frock, the buttons undone at the top and the bottom, and her legs were visible to the thigh as she knelt in the sand, a faint down of blonde hair. She wasn't wearing a bra, and I remember the dip of her breasts when she leaned forward. But she was wearing pants; they were red like her dress, and your trunks. They were red and expensive and once bought to please me, lace-panelled and silky, but fading, washed out, as old as her dress, whilst I was in shorts, a T-shirt and sandals, all of them new. Ruth had chosen my clothes before we came out on that holiday; she had taken me round shops I wouldn't normally go into. I hadn't worn sandals or shorts since I was a boy, and hadn't thought they would suit me. But Ruth liked my legs – they were skinny like yours – and she said I ought to show them more often. So I wore my new shorts, longer and baggier than yours, and that day Ruth wore her red pants. Her red knickers; on a lady or girl, they're called knickers.

It was Ruth who picked up my camera. She told you to stand close beside me, for it was our legs that she wanted. She called them my best feature, and the picture is cropped at my waist, my hand on your shoulder. And so later, when I took up the camera, I said now it was my turn; I would capture the feature I liked best about her. She was scooping a moat around the sandcastle we'd built. Bent forward, the sun slipped down her dress, and I focused the lens on her breasts. She looked up and poked out her tongue – she didn't smile – and no, you weren't standing beside her, not in that picture, but there were so many others; the film by then was almost used up. An hour earlier, as you'd taunted and run from the surf, I'd walked backwards, focusing, snapping, and winding. And some time before that I'd sat you on the steps of our caravan, Ruth looking out from the window, my shoes and sunhat and glasses arranged on the grass. In the morning, as you'd walked along the

187

track into town, holding Ruth's hand and sharing her umbrella, I'd called out to you suddenly and then taken a snapshot. I'd crouched by the carousel in the funfair and waited for your horse to dip into view. I'd used a flash in the amusement arcade, and leaned over the balcony in the swimming-pool. And then later, much later – not that day, or even the next – there would be one more, the final shot on that film and the last I would take, the aperture closing around you, and then darkness.

But you were already absent – your clothes kicked out of the way – when I took that photo of Mummy leaning over our sandcastle. It had been raining all night and for most of the morning. The sand was soft and fine at the surface, damp and grainy a few inches beneath. You had gone up the slope of the beach to gather some shells, some decoration to place round the turrets. Which was my idea, Euan. I'd passed you your bucket – that was all you would need – but still you'd insisted on taking your spade, your blue one. Perhaps you'd already decided on some other plan, perhaps it was then that you'd decided to hide. I would be along in a minute, I'd told you, lifting my camera, removing the lens-cap. I had said I would find you – those were my words – and I'd said you weren't to go far. So it wasn't your fault, you weren't being naughty. I had said *find*; so of course you'd think *hide*. You were five and a half.

A minute isn't a long time, more than enough for one photo. Another minute slipped by, and then a few more – nine or ten, maybe fifteen – but I didn't forget you, I held you somewhere in mind as I lay on my back in the sand at Ruth's side. You were always hiding, Euan, and sometimes we would ignore you. Eventually you'd come out to join us. But I wasn't ignoring you then; I always intended to follow. In a minute, I'd said. The sand was warm and I began to feel drowsy. Ruth sat across me, one hand splayed out on my chest, and she drank the last of our water. I narrowed my eyes to the glare of sunlight. I smoothed my hands on her arms and she lowered herself to her elbows, her chin touching mine, and she kissed me. She rolled on to her back. I had an erection. We held hands, and I listened to the sounds of our holiday, the gulls and the hush of the sea, the cracking of the breeze in a windbreak, a bellying deckchair. There was a motorboat, murmuring voices, a dog barking, and the noises of children. But I couldn't hear you, your voice amongst theirs. It was the dog that disturbed me. I'd better go and see what he's up to, I said.

It didn't take long, another few minutes. I set out for the cliffs, scuffing through the soft sand, and if I noticed the girl, it was only in passing, for I was looking for you, Euan; your red trunks and dark hair. Our beach was busy that afternoon – as crowded as it ever became that far down from the pier – and there were so many children. I scanned the deckchairs and windbreaks, and I saw a few faces I recognised – other people we knew from the caravans – but they didn't look up and I didn't approach them. I shielded my eyes and looked out to the sea, the lethargic roll of the waves and the shimmering air, the scatter of figures on the shoreline. And of course you weren't to be seen. I hadn't expected you would be, but for a brief moment then I felt fearful – something disturbed me – and I glanced towards Ruth. She had turned onto her belly and she seemed to be sleeping. Her dress was bunched at her buttocks and her legs were splayed out on our blanket. Everything remained as it was; and when I turned again to the cliffs I saw the girl clearly, thirty yards in the distance. I registered then what she doing, and vaguely it seemed I'd known all along. You would have called her a big girl, Euan. She was fourteen – a one and a four – and her name, I learned later, was Chloe. She was a teenager, and she was digging in the sand at the base of the cliffs – frantically digging – and her dog was flapping its tail, edging closer then back, crouching and barking. She was wearing a yellow jersey, V-necked and sleeveless, and a pair of mauve shorts, some white plastic sandals. Her dog was an old one. His snout was grizzled, his belly distended, but he was large and excited, and I'm sure you wouldn't have liked him. His name, I remember, was Toby.

There was an immediate clench of adrenaline, my heart suddenly lurching, and yet still, for a few paces more, I resisted the impulse to run. I looked all around me, making sure that no one was watching, confirming your absence from all that I'd seen. And then I was sprinting, as fast as I could through the drag of the sand. I yelled out Ruth's name. I stumbled, got up, and it was then that I found you. You were hiding. You had tunnelled into one of the hollows at the base of the cliffs. There were tucks and folds there just deep enough for you to crouch down in. But you hadn't wanted to crouch; you had used your spade and gone further. The sand was damp – it had been raining all night and for most of the morning – and a section of cliff had crumbled, collapsed on to you, leaving a tall shallow groove, a pile of debris. I saw your legs, and I knew their size, their shape, and your ankles. They were skinny like mine. You were buried face down, and your toes had turned blue. I fell to my knees – Chloe kneeling beside me – and no, I said nothing to her. I began digging, and dug with both hands, but Chloe's dog was excited. He jumped at my back. I felt his claws through my shirt, and I shouted; I swung out an arm. Chloe dragged him away then. She held him by the collar and watched me. She was crying, I remember, and some other people were coming towards us, Ruth somewhere amongst them. The dog was yelping, slavering wildly, and I shouted at Chloe. I told her to ring for an ambulance – there was a phone at the top of the cliffs, up the rickety steps – and as she ran off, the dog leaping beside her, I heard Ruth yelling your name, her panic and fury, and the echo of her voice skirling back from the cliff-face. Then she too was tearing with her hands at the sand, the rocks and fossil-strewn scree. There wasn't much room. Other hands were trying to help us, our arms and elbows colliding. Some more sand collapsed from above. And when at last we got past your trunks I took hold of your legs in my arms and I dragged you. I panicked too; I didn't know what I was doing. Your body juddered over the ground. Your head bumped as it came, and it was then that Ruth wailed, a sound I'd last heard in the hospital, five and a half years before.

The digging had taken five minutes, ten, I have no idea, but it was a very long time, Euan, long enough for you to leave us, for your heart to stop beating. I turned you over. Your lips and fingers were blue, your hair claggy with sand, your eyelashes. There was a plug of blood-clotted sand in your nose and I plucked it away. And then I did what I knew, the ABC I'd learned in my lessons – the airway, breathing, circulation. I tilted your head back and opened your mouth. I pushed a forefinger to the back of your throat, and as I scooped for the sand there, finding nothing, I remembered – a fleeting image, a reflex of memory – a moment when you were eighteen months old and taking a bath in your tub. There was a moulded tray in the rim of the bath where the water would gather. You liked to drink from it. And that evening, as I glanced to the television, I thought I saw you suck up the sliver of soap that lay there. You seemed to be choking, and immediately I swept you out of the water. I forced my finger into your mouth. There was a blockage; I was sure I could feel it. I jabbed and clawed with my fingernail, and then turned you on to your front and patted hard on your back. But your cries were too clear – the soap, I realised, was still in the water. By then you were screeching, and my hands were shaking. I wrapped you in a towel, and cradled and rocked you; I bit hard on the towel to stop myself crying. I had panicked, as I always would. And I was panicking still. I thought I might cry. But you made no sound at all. You weren't breathing, and you hadn't a pulse.

I pinched your nostrils together and put my mouth over your mouth – sand gritting my tongue, my lips – and I gave to you all the breath that I had. Your chest rose. I breathed into you again, and felt your neck for a pulse, but still there was nothing. I found the end of your breastbone, and measured two finger widths up, my nails broken, flaps of torn skin on my knuckles. I locked my hands together, one on top of the other, and pressed down with the heel of my hand. But that was too much; your chest was too small. I pressed with only one hand, and released, and slumped back on my heels; I counted one-and-two, and did it again. Sweat stung my eyes. I counted fifteen compressions, another two breaths, and then I returned to your chest. I did what I knew, what I thought I remembered, forcing your heart to circulate blood, transferring my oxygen, counting fifteen then two, fifteen then two. And all the time Ruth was saying your name, pathetic and pleading, holding your face in her hands to stop the loll of your head as I thrust down on your chest, until at last I told her to take over, to copy what I had done: pinch your nose, seal her mouth over yours, blow hard and evenly. But she was too hasty, she wanted to start even whilst I was pumping, and then she didn't do it quite right, and I snapped at her, I shouted. I shouted at Mummy as I had shouted at Chloe.

The ambulance was a long time in coming – it felt like a long time – and I remember Chloe came back to us, though not now with her dog. She was panting, and seemed frightened, but she said she had phoned. And I kept going, my shirt clammy with sweat, the backs of my knees. My new sandals bit into my feet. My arms and shoulders were aching, and I felt a hand on my elbow. The man was bearded, older than me, and he offered to take over; he said he knew what to do. But I shook my head, Euan. I wouldn't allow him, for I was your father; it was my job to help you. The other people were standing now at a distance. Some couldn't watch, but how could they leave? The parents had ushered their children away. Then I heard the man asking Chloe where she had rung from, and what directions she'd given. She pointed to the top of the cliffs, our caravan site, and admitted that she'd left no one to meet them. Come on then, he said, and led her away by the arm. They started to trot. I heard their feet on the steps. I took all of this in, and I continued to count – fifteen compressions, two breaths – and I heard the sounds of our beach, the speedboat passing and turning, the sea. I noticed the bruise on your chest where I was pressing, and the limp jerk of your arms and your legs, the dusky cast to your face. I saw Ruth wiping her eyes with the back of her hand, the snot from her nose. But I wasn't crying, Euan. I thought that I might, but I couldn't. It wasn't something I did. And though I knew it was hopeless, that you'd already gone, still I wouldn't give up. I kept hoping. I couldn't imagine a future without you, as I couldn't then keep from my mind the images – the random memories – of how you had been. Your life passed before me, Euan, the life you were leaving, all the stuff I'd recorded, and which you would never have time for.

I saw all of that, and I saw the paramedics hurrying towards us, their blue and yellow jumpsuits, and the weight of their bags bumping into their legs. And no, the ambulance didn't come down to the beach, but we would see it later, a real one. It had a blue light and a siren, and it was parked up near our caravan. That would be after the ambulancemen had got your heart beating, independent of me. They took over, and I had no purpose then but to stand and look on. I reached out for Ruth, and she came to me slowly, desolate, lost to herself and to me, unable to watch. I smelled the sweat in her hair, and the sourness of her breath, but she wasn't crying then; she was shaking. The men did what they knew, what they'd been trained for, and I remember the pads they clapped on to your chest, and the shout of *Stand clear*! The shock made you jolt, Euan; jerk up from the ground. The sound was hollow, a thwack like a slap, and Ruth glanced at you then, looked briefly. The men were watching a monitor. They slid a tube down your throat, and connected that to a cylinder. One of them squeezed a bag, then did some compressions. They stepped up the voltage; they got your heart beating. But you had already gone, Euan. You died because you'd stopped breathing. You died of compression asphyxia. The pressure of your burial had squashed up your chest so hard it couldn't expand. Your lungs had failed. The respiratory centres in your brainstem had starved; they hadn't had enough oxygen and so you had died. You could not be revived. But the heart is a machine, Euan; shocked into working, it carried on regardless. For three days more, it kept pumping. The coroner recorded a verdict of accidental death, and the newspaper called it a Tunnelling Tragedy. *Couple's Agony At Tunnelling Tragedy*. Your picture appeared on the television. Many people came to the funeral. We had you cremated. And no, you cannot come back now; it isn't okay to come back now.

TWENTY-NINE

There ought to have been rain, darkness, cold; it should have been winter. Instead there was sunshine, the scents and noises of summer. Our windows stayed open to the sounds of our neighbours, their kitchens and gardens, the traffic beyond. The light softly faded, returned. One hot day succeeded another. The mail kept arriving. The clock at Ruth's bedside kept pace with the seconds, the minutes and hours, but time had no use for you now, and meant nothing to me. When to wash, dress or eat; the simplest act would defeat me. I wandered into rooms only to forget why I'd gone there. I stumbled drunk into bed in the early hours of the morning, and woke in a sweat soon after, woke repeatedly all night, and then again as Ruth dressed. I would listen to her tread on the boards and the slide and clunk of the drawers, her coat-hangers jangling, and stare into the pillows and bedclothes, the sunlight on her jewellery, and feel only the blanketing weight of my loss, another day to come in your absence. Heavy-limbed and hung-over, I closed my eyes, curled into myself, and sank again into numbness, forgetting.

But of course I could not forget. My thoughts, my memory, were independent of me. I saw your sandals, your ankles, the fall of the cliff on your legs. I saw your blue toes and fingers. I remembered the sunburn on your shoulders, and the cold hard press of your bedframe, the tube in your mouth and the gaps in your teeth, the sensors and wires and banks of machines, but often also my mother, propped up on her pillows, smiling feebly across the distance between us, extend-ing her arm. There was my father's grip on my shoulder, and the single sharp crease of her frown, the dry white skin on her lips. Repeatedly I saw a cream-coloured ambulance – the driver removing his cap, raking a hand though his hair – and then a nurse striding before me, splay-footed, her shoes as clumpy and black as a man's. I saw these things, and I found myself shaking. My neck and legs began prickling with sweat; sudden pains clenched my stomach, my chest. The light was too bright, and sometimes I thought I would vomit. Often I cried. Eventually the numbness returned.

There ought to have been silence, the hush of snow falling, everything frozen, but still the cars continued to pass in our street, the footsteps and voices. I heard the lawnmowers and telephones, scudding footballs and children – always the children – and felt not just your absence from our house, the life we had made, but also from those noises outside, your part in all that. Most afternoons, too, I spent long hours in bed. Half naked, exhausted, I lay beneath my tangle of sheets and listened to Ruth's movements downstairs – the constant shufflings and knocks, doors opening and closing, her feet in the hallway – and felt as if eavesdropping on some other life, remote and unconnected with mine. Descending the stairs, I would find her scrubbing the stains from the carpets, the sofas and chairs. In every room except yours she took down the curtains, washed them by hand, and repositioned the furniture. She dragged out the cooker and scoured the dirt from the skirting behind it. But however much I wished she would stop, leave these things as they were, still I said nothing. I never complained, just as Ruth never once mentioned my smoking, or the amount I was drinking, the hours I spent idle. I heard her crying, as she must have heard me, and knew I could not go near her. In the evenings we prepared our meals separately, not talking, our eyes rarely meeting. Often we ate in different rooms.

Ruth returned to work at the end of the summer, and the house then was too empty, too quiet. I could not sit indoors, but I could not leave either. Daily I walked to the off-licence, two streets over from ours, and I always left the door open, then hurried straight back. I sat with my beers in the garden, gazing down at our vegetables, the tiny plot we called our allotment. I had bought all we needed in April – the seeds and tubers and bulbs – and I'd lifted the turf, dug over the soil, erected the bean-poles, but the arrangement was yours, the random clusters and clumps, nothing in rows. You'd planted a plastic windmill to scare off the birds, and when the first weeds had appeared you'd insisted these were our carrots, and so for a while I'd left them. But already in May your interest was waning, and when finally I'd plucked out the shoots you had played unconcerned on the lawn. A week or so later I'd found you digging a hole in the soil, unearthing our seeds, looking for insects. It was your garden, you'd told me; you could dig where you wanted. And I hadn't argued; I'd lost interest too. But even despite our neglect the vegetables had grown, and as the weeks passed now in your absence I sat in the creaking shade of the apple tree – pestered by midges, smoking and drinking – and I watched them. The grass returned, the crops bolted, and slowly the weeds began to take over, but I touched nothing. Your bucket and spade remained where you'd left them. Your windmill fitfully stirred.

It was some time in September, one evening at dusk, the rain soft and persistent, when Ruth came down from the house with my anorak. I looked at her blankly. My hair was matted, water streaking my face. Why don't you come in now? she said, and I nodded, then returned my gaze to our garden. She laid the coat by my side on the bench. She tucked her hands under her arms, and I glanced at her. Please, Paul, she said; can't you come in now? We have to talk, she said; don't you think we should talk, Paul? But I didn't reply. Say something, she said, and I stared at your spade, almost lost in the leaves. About what? I murmured. Us, she said; everything, whatever. And I shrugged. I pulled the ring from a beercan. There isn't an *us*, I said finally; is there? Not any more. There's nothing, I said, and she shook her head, looked away from me. She took a breath. A few moments later she turned and walked back up the lawn. I flapped the anorak open and sheltered beneath it, drew it over my head – how we would at the seaside, the rain pittering on to the plastic – and I pinched out some tobacco, laid it onto a paper, spreading and tamping, untangling the knots.

When later I came up to the house I saw her sitting in the dark of the dining room, the white of her blouse and her face. She seemed to be eating, her head propped on one hand. Perhaps she was reading. The side door was still open. In the kitchen I kicked off my shoes and left them to dry by the radiator. I wiped my neck with a tea-towel, my hair and my face. I switched on the kettle. My jeans were heavy with damp, my sweater and socks, and I took them off too. I let them lie where they fell. I relit my cigarette, and shivering, I stood by the sink and stared out of the window. My gaze met the wall of the neighbouring house. The bricks had deep striations running diagonally and the mortar was grainy. On the slats of the fence in between us I saw a faint blue tracing of chalk, the drawing you'd made of our house, and my eyes withdrew to the plant on our window-ledge, the leaves browned at the tips, the pot green with mould. A plastic marker was stuck in the soil, and I stared at the symbols, the half-shaded sun, the temperature gauge. I dipped the end of my cigarette in the washing-up bowl and exhaled a long breath of smoke. I let go of the stub and watched it float in the water, the paper darkening, unfurling, the strands of tobacco slowly dispersing. The kettle came to the boil and clicked off. The fridge began humming. I placed my hands on the drainer and looked down at my veins, the fat whorls of my knuckles, the nicotine stains, and then like a cough, like a hiccup, I found I was sobbing. I felt the slow involution as I folded in on myself. I sank to the floor and curled into a corner. I heard the noise I was making, and the drag of Ruth's chair, her footsteps. She paused in the doorway and switched on the light. Don't Paul, she said, and came forward, hunkered beside me. She placed a hand on my shoulder, her grip listless, a shake. She said something – something she ought to – and touched my hair, cupped her hands round my face. She tried to lift me. She said I wasn't to do this. Her eyes were wide and she too was starting to cry. I opened my arms and she held me; she clasped my head to her shoulder. She was warm and smelled of her office, dimly of perfume. Her lips when we kissed were flaked with dry skin. My breath tasted of ash. I fumbled to unfasten her blouse and she helped me. I pushed up her bra and closed my mouth on her breast. My left arm was beneath her, the floor cold and hard. And kneeling, I dragged down her tights, her pants. She held on to my hips, her nails digging in, her eyes tightly closed, and we fucked rawly, a knot of clothes on the linoleum. Our heads were pressed to the cooker. It was the last time. Afterwards we parted, slunk away from each other. Ruth went upstairs to the shower; later she returned to the dining room. I sat and started at the television, the volume turned down, and that night, as we lay in bed without touching, not talking, I heard again and again my sobs in the kitchen, the rasp in Ruth's breath, and the only word she had spoken, a hot whispered *Euan*.

THIRTY

A few streets in from the sea there is silence. I hear my own breath and the crump of my feet on the snow. Meltwater trickles into the drains; heavy drips fall from the trees, the lampposts and railings. A motorbike shifts gears in the distance, but the roads around here are deserted. The grey metal shutters are down on the shops. Even the mini-mart, just facing the bus depot, is shortly to close. A uniformed woman comes out as I enter, unhooks the day's papers and brings them inside, props the rack by the counter and shivers. She says I've just made it, and clicks the snub on the door, flips over the sign in the window. There's a flattened box for a doormat, slushy prints up the aisles. A younger woman is counting the cigarettes, tapping down the packs with a biro. She writes on a clipboard and gives me a smile. The lighting is garish, and the warmth makes me blush. When I speak – my voice thick and nasal – it sounds as though I am shouting. I buy another half-bottle of whisky, a pouch of tobacco, some more Rizlas and tissues, but I cannot look to her face. The clock behind her shows 5:55. There are sandwiches on display in a cabinet, chilled pasties and pies, and though it occurs to me now that I'm hungry, and ought to buy food, I want only to return to the cold, the darkness outside. I slip the whisky into my pocket. The other woman is waiting. She unfastens the latch on the door and holds it wide open. Night, love, she says as I go.

The tiny depot is parked up with buses, all of them empty. A drinks machine gleams from the staffroom. The ticket office is shut, the windows pasted with posters, special-offer excursions, and as I look for our timetable I remember the last time we came here. It was June, the first night of our holiday, and we'd left Ruth behind in the caravan, unpacking our bags and our shopping, laying fresh sheets on the beds. In a restaurant called the Asteria we had eaten roast chicken and chips, and then gone to the children's show in the Hippodrome, and passed half an hour on the pier. Afterwards, waiting for our bus home, you had sat on the bench by the staffroom, clutching your programme. An old man was sitting there with you, dressed in a black suit and tie, a thick woollen coat. His whole body was shaking, his face livid, unshaven, and it seemed he could not breathe except through his cigarette. With each inhalation his shaking increased. I murmured your name and shook my head because you were staring. Then he coughed, or tried to, his face tense with the effort, his tremors stilled for that moment. Finally he hawked some phlegm at the pavement and smeared his mouth on his sleeve. He pointed to some graffiti behind him. I sat here yesterday, he told me; watched them doing that. Two lads and a girl. Disgusting things they write. Filth. And if you say anything to them, you only get more of the same. I suppose so, I said. He brought the cigarette to his lips, drew deeply, and then looked at you sternly. Are you a good boy? he demanded, but you didn't reply. You came and stood by me, wrapped your arms round my legs. Yes, I said; yes, he is a good boy, and I ruffled your hair. What age will he be now? the man said, but you pulled on my arm, dragged me away before I could answer. Don't tell him, Daddy, you whispered.

Our bus now is approaching. It's a yellow-liveried seven-teen-seater called the Flying Banana, and it stops over the road, its engine still thrumming. As I step from the kerb I hold out my hand to guide you; I glance left and right. The driver – hook-nosed, his moustache curling into his sideburns – is one we know well. He has a routine. We have seen it before. He takes my money, but fumbles as he returns my small change. And a fivepenny piece, he says, then appears to drop it. No, no, hold on, there's one sprouted legs, either that or wings, legs or wings, one or the other. He winks, but I have no inclination to smile; I take my coins and sit three rows behind him. The seats on this

207

side are singles. You always insisted we should sit separately, and I wasn't allowed to look back; we had to pretend we were strangers. There are no other passengers. The driver whistles as he drives, and lets out a low growl each time he accelerates. You once told me you liked him; he was your favourite.

A bottle lists as we turn, rolls under the seats at the back. We pass a long line of hotels – Windy Shore, Tudor Gables, Ocean Dawn, Gable End – and then a Shell service station, a yellow scallop on red, after which the town is behind us. The bus illuminates the dark twists in the road, the swirl of snow falling. I clear my nose and take out a cough sweet. I press my face to the window and gaze out on the snow-covered fields, the trees haggard and stunted, like inverted brooms, shaped by the wind from the sea. The engine noise changes, deepens and coarsens, and then we are rising and I remember the day of your cremation, the long slow climb to the chapel and the hum of our car, its smell of warm leather. In the smoked-glass screen behind the driver I glimpsed Ruth's reflection, her blankness. Our hands were clasped on the seat – clasped so long they'd become numb – and though your coffin was small, I wished then it could be smaller, take its place in the space between us. The road was narrow and steep and as we ascended I felt my back pressing into the seat; I felt the weight of my breathing, sweat prickling my chest. I thought I was going to be sick. There were high mud banks on each side of us, Victorian lampposts, tall conifers. I lowered my window and sank back in the breeze.

I closed my eyes and inhaled. The car levelled and stopped, and for some time I could not get out. It was Polly who opened my door. I remember she offered her hand, and I gazed at her black dress, her black hat and veil. We had said that there shouldn't be black, but your funeral was hers; she had organised everything. She was good at such things, and we hadn't had the strength to resist her. But I shook my head then; I refused to get up. Ruth ducked out before me. She touched my knee and murmured my name. She waited. Others were waiting behind her, and finally I nodded. I let her take both my hands. She helped me to stand. She ought to be here with me now. Our stop is arriving, and I don't think I can move. Perhaps the driver will continue, take me on to the next town. But he slows, and calls out; he leans over and looks round; and as I pull myself up I realise how drunk I've become. Slowly I make my way down the aisle, holding on to the poles, the chair-backs, and as the doors flip open the driver says, Thanking you; happy Christmas, mind how you go. I step out into darkness, empty fields and tumbling sky, and I watch the bus leaving. A couple of cars rush by me, and then there is nothing. Snow peppers my coat. Our caravan site is over the road.

THIRTY-ONE

It was lunchtime, your third day in the hospital, and as we sat in our grey bucket seats, one on each side of your bed, I held on to your fingers and blankly gazed at your monitors – the flickering numbers and waveforms – and then looked to the alphabet frieze on your wall, the posters and drawings, and the red-ribboned rosette that was pinned up beside them. *Euan*, it said; *for bravery*. I clenched my jaw and looked down. Nothing moved but the steady rise and fall of your chest. The ventilator behind me hissed and sucked as it breathed for you, and shaking my head, I wished that all of this could be over – the tubes and wires and machines – for your story now was make-believe, Euan. You were not brave, and you would not be waking. One consultant already had tested you, and soon enough another would confirm what she'd found, that however hard you were prodded or pinched, and whatever was shone or squirted into your eyes, or placed down your throat, you could not be hurt, for you had no life left in you, no reflex or response. Your brainstem was dead. And when Ruth again began weeping, and scraped back her chair, I went across to the rosette and carefully unpinned it. I guided her out through the grey double doors, down the wide stairwells and corridors, and we returned once more to the Parents' Room, no longer quite parents. The heat in there was stifling, and smelled of us, the days and hours we'd spent waiting. I laid your rosette on our bed and opened a window. The sea glimmered blue in the distance, and I stared down at the gardens, the deep shade of the hedges, and quietly then I suggested we should go for a walk, perhaps find somewhere to eat. Ruth nodded, not looking at me, and picked up her purse.

We didn't go far, a couple of streets, and I remember the traffic as we came from the hospital, the buffeting noise and the sunshine. Ruth's skirt flapped up in the breeze and some builders stopped working to watch her. She folded her arms on her chest and walked with head bowed, her face obscured by her hair, and it wasn't until we came to a crossing – the Hurricane a short distance beyond it – that I saw she was still crying. Clumsily then I tried to embrace her, but she didn't want to be held, stiffly waited until I let go. She turned and hurried over the road, went into the pub before me. The lounge had not altered, and there were no other people. I looked around at the red leather benches and stools, the paintings of planes on the walls, and gently I asked if she was sure about this, if she wouldn't rather keep walking. I touched her shoulder. Please, Paul, she sighed; could you just let me be for a minute? She blew her nose and sat down; she placed her purse on the table. I took it through to the pool room. There was a vending machine in the corner, and I bought a packet of cigarettes.

We drank whiskies, and though eventually Ruth reached for my cigarettes, and tipped one from the pack, she did not smoke it, but turned it around in her fingers and quietly said, They remind me of your dad, Paul. And I nodded; I picked up my glass. Don't you think you should phone him? she said. There's no point, I exhaled; he won't be interested, it won't register. It will, she replied; I think it will, Paul. But I shook my head. I doubt it, I murmured, and stared out to the yard, the beer kegs stacked up by the wall, the dustbins. I finished my drink. Ruth opened her purse and took my glass from me. I'll get you another, she said, and as she went up to the bar I stubbed out my cigarette, ground it into the ashtray, and thought then of the first time we took you to see him. You were four months old, and he was smoking as we came through the door, his cigarette half hidden behind him, cupped in the palm of his hand. He led us into the living room, a fug of smoke in the air, and I lifted the latch on a window, pushed a chair near it. Ruth sat with you in the draught. She smelled your nappy, and as I slipped your changing bag from my shoulder I heard the snap of his lighter. You've just put one out, Dad, I said. What's that? he asked me. You've only just finished one, I told him. No I haven't, he replied, and watched as Ruth knelt down on the carpet, absorbing every detail, the rise of her hem on her thighs, the dip of her neckline. She laid a fresh nappy beneath you, and suddenly then he started to cough, hacking into his fist, unable to stop. He went from the room and ran the taps in the kitchen. We sat and listened to the noise he was making. We heard it again when we went up to bed; we heard it repeatedly all weekend.

My other grandpa, you called him, the one who was poorly and lived far away, who couldn't come to our house. He was not playful like Jim, didn't tickle or chase you, and of course he never told stories, or listened to yours. He found your presence a nuisance it seemed, your constant activity and chatter, the attention you needed, for it was only ever Ruth that he wanted to talk to, until even that was too much, the exertion beyond him. His illness began I suppose in the year you were born, and steadily worsened each winter. He admitted first on the phone to a cold, and later, much later, to a bout of bronchitis. Finally it became emphysema, though he never would say so, at least not to me. By the time you were four he had smoked his last cigarette, and conceded to Ruth that he should have stopped sooner, but still he insisted on blaming his studio – the damage, he said, was due to his work, the gases and dust in the air, the chemicals he'd had to inhale. And Ruth nodded; she didn't bother to argue. He hadn't worked then in three years – his final sculptures abandoned – and I remember the effort he had just to keep breathing, his neck and shoulder muscles bulging, as though slowly shrugging, as if vaguely bewildered by the state he was in. He was sleepy, forgetful, his house as warm as my grandmother's had been, and like my grandmother he rarely went out, saw very few people. His life, like his lungs, had constricted, and the following year – the last time you saw him – he was barely able to rise from his chair. He couldn't breathe except through a machine, an oxygen concentrator rigged up in his hallway. Yards of plastic tubing led into his kitchen, his bedroom and living room. Two narrow prongs fed into his nose. His face was bloated, his eyes red and swollen. His chest was distended, and he spoke in a whisper. You said you didn't want to visit again; you thought he was scary. And I remember Ruth promised we'd see; perhaps next time Daddy could come on his own? She doubted he would live out that year.

We ought to get going, Ruth said to me now; it's almost two, and I nodded. I swallowed what remained of our whiskies, and picked up my cigarettes, and slowly we trailed back to the hospital, the sun sharp in our eyes and Ruth's hand holding mine. We did not speak, and came in by the car-park, the outpatients department, the lifts. We went first to your bedside, and I remember watching your nurses as they worked briskly around us, and the grey-coated auxiliary restocking your shelves, and thinking that soon another child would be lying where you lay, another just like you. Your last tests would be happening at four, and squeezing your leg, I got to my feet. I promised I would come for you later, and stumbled out through the doors, unsteady with drink, and returned to the Parents' Room. I slumped in an armchair, and Ruth came in behind me. She drew the curtains, and moved your rosette to my pillow. She lay down on the bed. The minutes continued to pass, and I felt myself drowsing, woke with a jolt as my chin touched my chest. Ruth's eyes were open, looking at me. You were snoring, she said. I ran a hand over my face, smelled the smoke on my fingers. Sorry, I said, and crossed to the wash-basin. Ruth sat up on the bed. I wasn't sleeping, she said. The clock on the wall showed half past three. I dried my hands and sat down. I stared at the curtains. Tiny points of light shone through the fabric; and we waited, alert only to the sounds from the corridor – the footsteps approaching, receding; the voices and laughter – and when at last the door opened it wasn't one of your nurses, or your consultant, but your grandfather Jim.

He arrived in a hurry – as if he thought he might save you; perhaps afraid that he'd already missed you – and then abruptly he stopped, a few paces into the room. Someone closed the door softly behind him. His shoulders sloped, his arms hung at his sides, and he started to cry, noiselessly, standing looking at Ruth. I rose from my chair and briefly I held him. I smelled his deodorant, and the air of outdoors released from his jacket. But it was Ruth that he wanted and I watched as they clung to each other, then took my cigarettes from the table, some coins from Ruth's purse, and quietly I left them. I wandered into the corridor. I breathed and exhaled. There were *No Smoking* signs everywhere, and I pushed through the doors to the stairwell, and descended six echoing flights – the concrete steps glossy with wear – and came to the lobby that led into the gardens. There was a payphone on the wall, a Perspex hood over it, and lighting a cigarette, I stood for a while in the doorway, looking out to the lawns, the benches and flower-beds, and rehearsed in my mind what I would say to my father. My voice would be steady and factual, sparing no detail. I would describe as much as there was, all I could think of, and though he might not want to know, still I would tell him. I'd remind him too of what he'd neglected, and what we were now losing. I would make him remember. But when at last I picked up the receiver, and punched out his number, I found myself shaking; I could not keep standing. I turned and crouched with my back to the wall. I lit another cigarette, and listened to the tone in my ear – repeatedly ringing – and it was then, for the first time since I was a boy, that I heard myself crying, uselessly saying his name, for he was not going to answer, and I knew I shouldn't have expected he would.

THIRTY-TWO

The wind now has relented, the snow thickly falling. The flakes
are luminous, silent. Looking up, I see them skewering towards
me, swarming out of the darkness. They settle over my coat,
crusting my chest and my shoulders; they melt on my lips.
Through the flickering whiteness our neighbours' caravans
appear and recede, their shapes vague, insubstantial. Beneath
the soft crush on the ground the grass is brittle and frozen. I
stumble on divots and tyre tracks, and find my way by
remembering – this far straight ahead, this distance across –
until our caravan bulks up before me. There's a skim of ice on
the windows. The roof is matted with snow, and there's snow
on the lumber box, the steps and the tow-bar. Ruth's car is not
here. I tug off my gloves and sweep the box clear with my arm.
The padlock is useless, open and frozen. I always meant to

replace it; and shivering, impatient, I drop it now to my feet. I lift back the lid. Inside are two gas-bottles, your buckets and spades, our fold-away table and chairs. I connect the supply pipe, release the valve on the gas. I let the lid fall and fumble through my pockets for keys. The lock takes a quarter turn anti-clockwise. The handle lifts upwards and the door opens out-wards. You never could manage to do this, however often we showed you.

The caravan rocks as I enter, the ornaments trembling, the cups on their hooks. There's a smell of damp bedding – the smell of every first day we spent here – and something sharper, more rancid. The doors are all closed, the curtains and blinds, and for a while I stand hunched in the darkness, carefully listening. The metal casing is silent, everything still. There's no sound but my own breath, the pulse in my ears. To my right is the broom-closet, your cabin beside it. The wall of our bed-room is somewhere before me. On my left is the passage, the toilet and shower stall, the kitchen units and stove, and cautiously I edge alongside them, patting the surfaces, feeling for the drainer, the rim of the sink. I reach across to the window. But the roller-blind won't open – the cord gives a little then locks – and I can't think now how to work it. I yank hard with both hands, but I seem to have jammed it, and defeated, self-conscious, I stand facing the living room, the end of our caravan. The dark is slowly revolving. I step on to the carpet, one arm extended before me, and grope for the curtains. I

220

bump into the table, take another three paces. My fingers sink into the fabric, my knees touch the bench, and exhaling, relieved, I pull the curtains wide open, drag them out to the corners. The snow shimmers white through the frost on the windows, and I look all around me, surveying the shapes and the shadows, all the low spaces. Everything remains just as it should be, the distances tiny, and I think then how happy you were here, secure in these dimensions. You only had to glance up and you would find us.

I crouch down by the fire and take out my lighter. The gas pops, a row of guttering flames, and I turn the setting to *max*. There's a lamp above to my left, another behind me, two more in the passage. The mantles hiss as they brighten, the sound soft and continuous. The last dark shapes resolve into towels, discarded jumpers and cushions, and there are toys on the floor, one of Ruth's compacts, the shrivelled peel of a tangerine. I have thrown nothing away here; I have not even tidied. The finger-smudges in the dust may be yours. The mud on the carpet may have come from your sandals. There's a carton of milk on the drainer, yellowed and sour. The plates are un-washed. Beneath the sink our binbag is full, the sliding doors open, and I shove the carton in the bag, tie a knot in the drawstring. And then shaking, clumsy with drink and the cold, I begin to unbutton my coat, squinting down at my fingers. I flap the snow from my shoulders, watch it drop to the lino. I clear my nose on some kitchen roll. There are doors all around me, cupboards and closets and cabins, and methodically I open each one in turn, scanning the dimness inside, snapping them shut. But your room remains undisturbed. I stand for some moments before it – the pale wood veneer, the alphabet stickers spelling your name – and though I raise a hand to the doorknob, I find I cannot go in there.

I return instead to the fireplace and kneel down on the carpet. I roll a cigarette and break the seal on my bottle; I empty my pockets. There's my wallet and cough-sweets and tissues, and your flower from Charlie, a patch in the shape of a heart, a flint shaped like a bird-skull. I lay them out on the hearth, and take a light from the flames. I pick up the hagstone and turn it around in my fingers. On the table behind me is our collection of pebbles with holes in, the dish shallow and wide, the largest I ever managed to throw, but our smaller earthenware bowls – the ones for our periwinkles, our cowries and tellins – sit now on a shelf in your cabin, and soon enough I may have to retrieve them. Ruth could yet be arriving, and perhaps she will be bringing your casket, your ashes, for it was her idea that we should deposit them here, somewhere close to our caravan, on this day, your birthday. We would make a memorial, a small cairn of hagstones and seashells. That was what we agreed in July, in the days after your funeral, and though she may since have forgotten, it does seem to me now that she'll have been to our house, as she said on the phone that she would. She will have looked to the pinboard, and read the note that I left her.

And if she is late, it's because she has worked. Today, as on every other day, she will have been to her office.

The heat from the fire is scorching. I pull off my hat and my scarf and lean back on a bench. Cold air descends from the windows, the vent by the ceiling, and I turn up my collar. I lift my gaze to your cabin, your stickers, and as I drink from my bottle I remember again your blank double doors, and our final journey towards them – Jim's arm around Ruth, one hand supporting her elbow – and the dread I felt then. I was carrying my camera, and wished that I'd left it, but a nurse had encouraged me; it was often a comfort, she'd said. She had squeezed my wrist gently. She stroked my arm as we filed into your room. The other nurses parted to admit us, then carried on with their work – whatever still remained to be done – and I hid the camera behind me. I placed it down on the floor, edged it away with my foot, and I went to stand at your bedside. I could not take your hand, only your fingers, for there was a plastic tap in the way, a thin tube looping over your thumb. A drip fed into your forearm; three sensors were attached to your ribs. The tube in your mouth forced back your lips, exposing the gaps in your teeth. A catheter entered your penis. Another went into your heart and emerged at your neck, the wires from there trailing up to a monitor. But soon all of this would be over. I felt a hand on my shoulder. There were seats for us to sit in, lined up by the wall. The lights were dimmed, and your ventilator switched off, your tube disconnected, and we watched as each wire and needle in turn was removed, the monitors unplugged, the drip-pole pushed back, the beeps and whistles gradually silenced. Your chest became still, deflated. Your last breath had gone, and you with it, but you didn't look dead, only sleeping, all energy spent, another day forgotten behind you. We came forward. Your cheeks were pink. There was a turquoise vein on your temple and I stroked it with the back of a finger, but my nail was broken; it left a small scratch. I leaned over and kissed it, your clammy forehead, and I smelled the staleness in your hair. Ruth gave me my camera, and I took a single picture, the final shot on that film, but I wanted only to hold you. I lifted you up from the bed, more heavy than I ever imagined. You weren't sleeping. You were lifeless, Euan; your arms and legs flaccid. Your head lolled and Ruth supported it. And slowly your face became pallid, more grey than white. The medics backed off, everything receded. They left us alone with you, and I held on to you tightly; I rocked you. I whispered into your ear. I lowered you back to the bed, and Ruth bent to embrace you, clutched your face to her breasts. She kissed your cheek, and folded your hands on your belly-button, your umbilicus. She did it carefully, precisely. She would not touch you again.

Time froze then. I remember the stillness. There was your stillness on the bed, your absolute deadness, but also the stillness that surrounded you, in which you'd taken your place. And until time resumed, until I became conscious again of the machines all around me, and the cold hard press of your bedframe, Ruth at my side and your grandfather hunched in his chair, I was there with you. Reality, awareness, returned in convulsions, racking sobs, reflexive spasms, many seconds or minutes apart, and as we trailed away, none of us touching, every moment and distance seemed longer. One foot in front of the other required concentration, an effort of will. We passed down corridors lined with children's paintings, hung with their mobiles. There were plastic tables and chairs, and boxes of toys, a rocking horse, piles of comics and books. There were children asleep in the wards. And as we came from that nursery world into the long stone-flagged tunnel that led to the Parents' Room, it seemed I heard your voice in me clearly – *where are you going?* – to which I hadn't an answer, for I was leaving you, Euan, no longer your father, and the velocity of that realisation winded me; it caused me to fall.

My whisky now is half empty, your hagstone warm in my hand. I crook my arms on the bench and drag myself upright. I place the stone in our bowl, and for a few moments then I stand over it, my weight pressing down on the table, my gaze shifting, unfocused. I am very drunk now, and when at last I step backwards I find I am lurching, tilting out to the passage. I steady myself on the cooker, and blunder ahead to your room. The door slams into the wall – the wooden partition – and of course there is nothing, no sense of you, not even your absence, only your things, your bunk and your boxes, a faint smell of mildew, and the noise of our caravan trembling. The air is cold on my face, and this is no more than a room. There are orange swirls in the carpet, pink drapes at the window, pale wood veneer on the cabinets. There's a stain in the curve of the ceiling, a leak in the roof. And then I don't know. I am turning, sweeping plates and cups from the drainer, knocking things over, whatever there is. I grab for the cushions and hurl them behind me. I swipe at the books on the window-ledge, and our souvenir ornaments, all the kitsch Ruth collected, and then I reach for our bowl. I slide it to the edge of the table, watch it tip as it falls. The pebbles tumble on to the carpet, scatter out to the corners. They cluck into each other, slowly settle in clutches, and soon after that there is silence. The bowl has broken cleanly. There are five or six pieces. I slump back on the bench, and stare down at the mess I have caused, and it seems my whole body is shaking, as if I was sobbing, but I am not crying, Euan; not now. Blankly I look to my hands, the nicotine stains on my fingers, and I reach then for my tobacco, my lighter and papers. I hold the pouch in my left palm, and trembling, I pinch out some more fibres. I draw them down the V of a Rizla.

The drive from our house takes ninety minutes, but of course there is snow, and darkness, patches of ice on the roads. And if Ruth has remembered – if my note was enough to remind her – she will have gone first to her own house and collected your casket. Perhaps she'll have spoken to Julie. She may have taken a shower, changed out of her workclothes. I suppose she'll have packed a bag for the night. She may have stopped off on the way. But I am tired now, Euan; I want only to be done with all this – the waiting, remembering, your unceasing questions. I want only to sleep now. I finish my cigarette and toss the butt to the hearthstone. I swill the taste from my mouth, and pick my way through the debris, the cushions and books on the floor, smashed vases and plates, and gently I close the door to your room. I extinguish the lights, slowly turn down the dials; I watch the flames faltering, the mantles gradually fading. Then I clear a space on the carpet. I drink again from my bottle, and gaze around at our caravan, the shadows and spaces, the stillness, and lowering myself to my knees, I turn off the fire. I wait a few moments, allow it to cool, then I raise the setting back up to *ign*. I wrap myself in my coat and lie down on my side. I reach across for your patch, close it into my fist. I pillow my head in my arms, and as I feel myself drowsing, no sound but the hiss of the gas, I remember Ruth's bedsit, the wind blustering outside and her oven door open, rain lashing the windows. It was Christmas, nine years ago, and she wore a pink cardigan. What do you want? I asked her; what would you most like to have? Oh, you know, she replied, her arms looped around me, her legs. We've discussed it, she said. There would be a Euan or a Jessica to begin with, and a place by the sea, a beach-hut, a caravan, somewhere to drive to at weekends. We never imagined a future without you, and I no longer supposed she would leave me. Perhaps soon she'll be here. I lift my head from my arms and blearily look to the windows, the dwindling

227

snow, and it does seem to me now that there's something, the barest disturbance, the faintest of noises. I try to reach for the gas, but it's too much, I let my arm fall. My face is pressed to the carpet, my eyes heavy and closing, but I can feel a vibration, the thrum of an engine. She will not find me like this. I force my eyes open, and heave myself to the fire. I close off the dial, turn on to my back. In a few moments more I will see the sweep of her headlights. I will hear her suspension, the wheels bumping over the divots and tyre tracks, and then her handbrake, the blip of the alarm, and the pause before she opens the door. She will smell the gas, and hurry back out to the box, disconnect the supply. She will hook open the door, and call out my name, cautious and frightened, and then feel her way towards me, kicking through the mess on the floor. And I will sit up; I will let her know that I am here, and she will open the windows, and sit heavily, as if she too has been walking all day. I will read many things into her expression, the tightness of her lips, the tautness in her jaw. She will be relieved, and wary; I suppose she will be angry. She will shiver perhaps, and tie a knot in her scarf, zip up her jacket, and we will sit in our customary silence, but I'll know that she is waiting. It's a long time since she has looked at me. She will expect me to speak; it is time that I spoke. And I will reach for my whisky, my tobacco and papers. I will begin to roll up a cigarette and then she will harden; she will get to her feet, and take her hat and gloves from her pockets. She will glance at me briefly, and make her way to the door.

She will leave me, and though I'll make no motion to stop her, the grief will seize hold of me then, catch and release me, and I will pull on my scarf, find my gloves and my hat, and I will follow her. She will be walking out to the cliffs, the rickety steps to the beach, and as she begins her descent I will light up my cigarette. The cold will flood in from the darkness, and I'll hold tight to the handrail, the boards layered with snow, crushed by Ruth's footsteps, and when I come to the sands I will keep my head down. I shall have to walk sideways, shielding my cigarette. I will inhale with my back to the wind. And when at last I glance round she will be there at the strand, dark against the dark of the sea, and perhaps you will be with her, holding on to her hand. For a moment I will hope so, but no, you won't be there. For you are dead now, Euan; and it is time that I left you, allowed you to go. Ruth alone will be facing out to that cold, which I have not managed today. And I will stand beside her, hunched into my coat. I will bring my cigarette to my lips, and taste the staleness of the ash. I will throw it aside, and pushing my hands in my pockets, I will lift my face and look out, Ruth's presence beside me. I will feel it, her closeness, the fact that she is there, and that will be all. It will be enough. The sea will be howling in the darkness, the white crests igniting.

ACKNOWLEDGEMENTS

My thanks are due to the Authors' Foundation and the Eastern Arts Board for financial assistance during the writing of this novel.

For their help and advice I would also like to thank Neil Taylor and Carole Welch; Chris Wright; Lynn and Phil Whitaker; Judy Coggon; the sculptors of Hardingham Workshops – Pete Blunsden, John Foster and Andy Sloan; and above all, Lynne Bryan.